WANTED:
Phatax, ruthless interplanetary criminal.

CRIME:
Kidnapping, theft.

WHEREABOUTS:
The planet Threefax.

YOUR MISSION:
[illegible]

Bantam Books in the
Be An Interplanetary Spy Series

#1 **FIND THE KIRILLIAN!**
by Seth McEvoy
illustrated by Marc Hempel
and Mark Wheatley

#2 **THE GALACTIC PIRATE**
by Seth McEvoy
illustrated by Marc Hempel
and Mark Wheatley

BE AN INTERPLANETARY SPY™ 1

FIND THE KIRILLIAN!

by Seth McEvoy
Illustrated by Marc Hempel
and Mark Wheatley

A
Byron Preiss
Book

ibooks
IBOOKS For Young Readers
Habent Sua Fata Libelli

Seth McEvoy, author, is an active member of the Science Fiction Writers of America; a video game designer and programmer; and is currently writing a critical study of the work of Samuel R. Delany.

Marc Hempel and Wark Wheatley, illustrators, joined forces in 1980 as Insight Studios to produce comics, illustrations, and graphic design. Marc Hempel has a degree in Painting and Illustration from Northern Illinois University. His work has appeared in *Heavy Metal*, *Epic Illustrated*, *Bop*, *Fantastic Films*, *Video Action*, and *Eclipse*. Mark Wheatley has a degree in Communications Arts and Design from Virginia Commonwealth University. His work has appeared in *Metal*, *Epic Illustrated*, Zebra Books and on Avalon Hill Games. Currently he and Marc are collaborationg on a graphic story series, *Mars*.

Ages 9 and up
Find the Kirillian!
978-1-59687-006-2

Special thanks to Judy Gitenstein, Laure Smith, Ron Buehl, Anne Greenberg, Ellen Steiber, Lucy Salvino, Laura Dirksen, Steve Stiles, Cariol Wheatley, and Ron Bell.

Cover art and book design by Marc Hempel
Mechanical Production by Insight Studios
Typesetting by Daystar Graphics

IBOOKS for Young Readers
www.ibooksinc.com
bricktower@aol.com

Introduction

You are an Interplanetary Spy. You are about to embark on a dangerous mission. On your mission you will face challenges that may result in your death.

You work for the Interplanetary Spy Center, a far-reaching organization devoted to stopping crime and terrorism in the galaxy. While you are on your mission, you will take your orders from the Interplanetary Spy Center. Follow your instructions carefully.

You will be traveling alone on your mission. If you are captured, the Interplanetary Spy Center will not be able to help you. Only your wits and your sharp spy skills will help you reach your goal. Be careful. Keep your eyes open at all times.

If you are ready to meet the challenge of being an Interplanetary Spy, **turn to Page 1.**

TOP SECRET

Enter your Interplanetary Spy ISBN number below:

If you are not sure, examine the back cover of the book.

Turn to Page 2

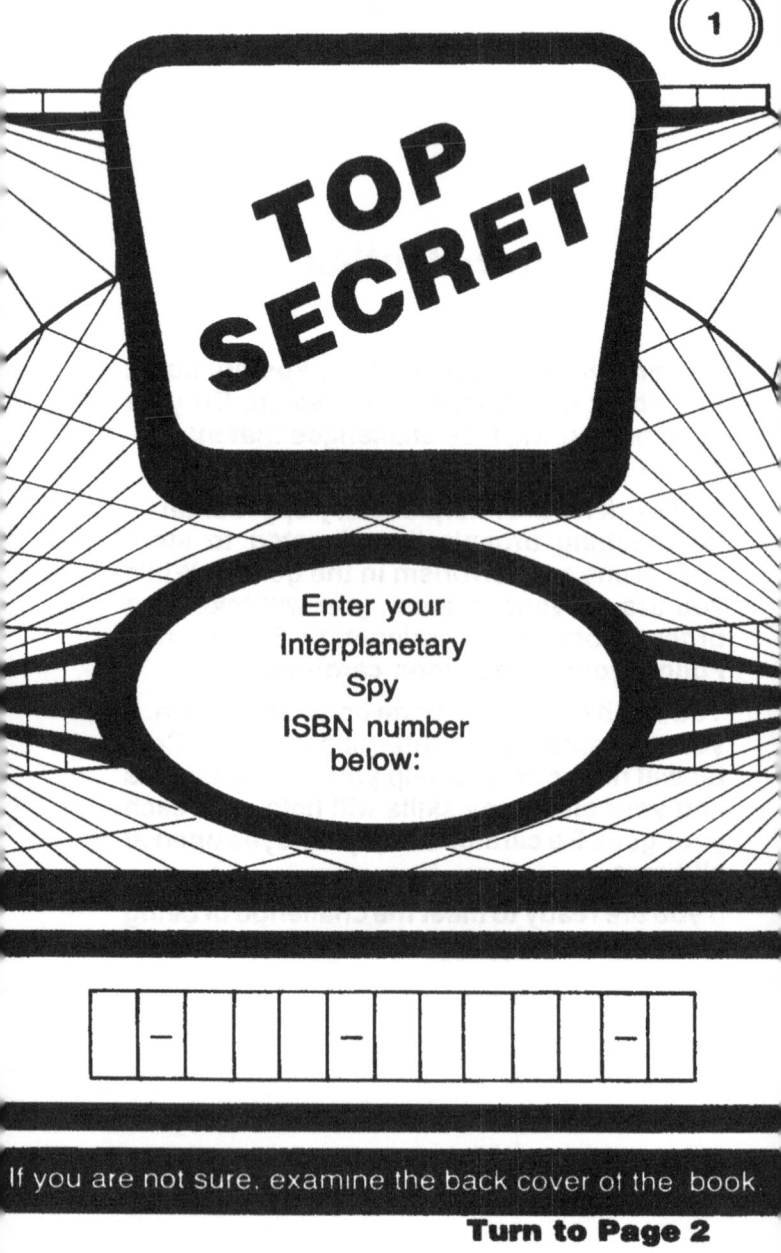

Welcome.

Your Mission is
to capture this
interplanetary
criminal: Phatax.

He is very dangerous. He is from the outlaw planet, Kirillia:

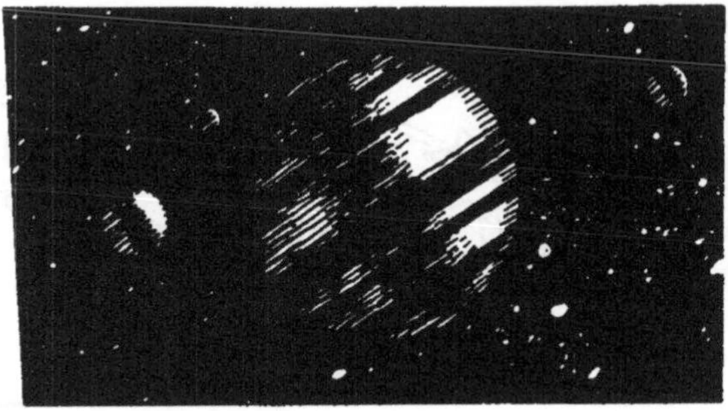

Phatax is ruthless. He has kidnapped Prince Quizon of the planet Alvare. Prince Quizon is the Keeper of the Royal Jewels of Alvare.

For more information, you must complete the Spaceport Maze.

Turn to Page 4

4

You arrive at the spaceport.
You must go through the maze and correctly enter your shuttlecraft.

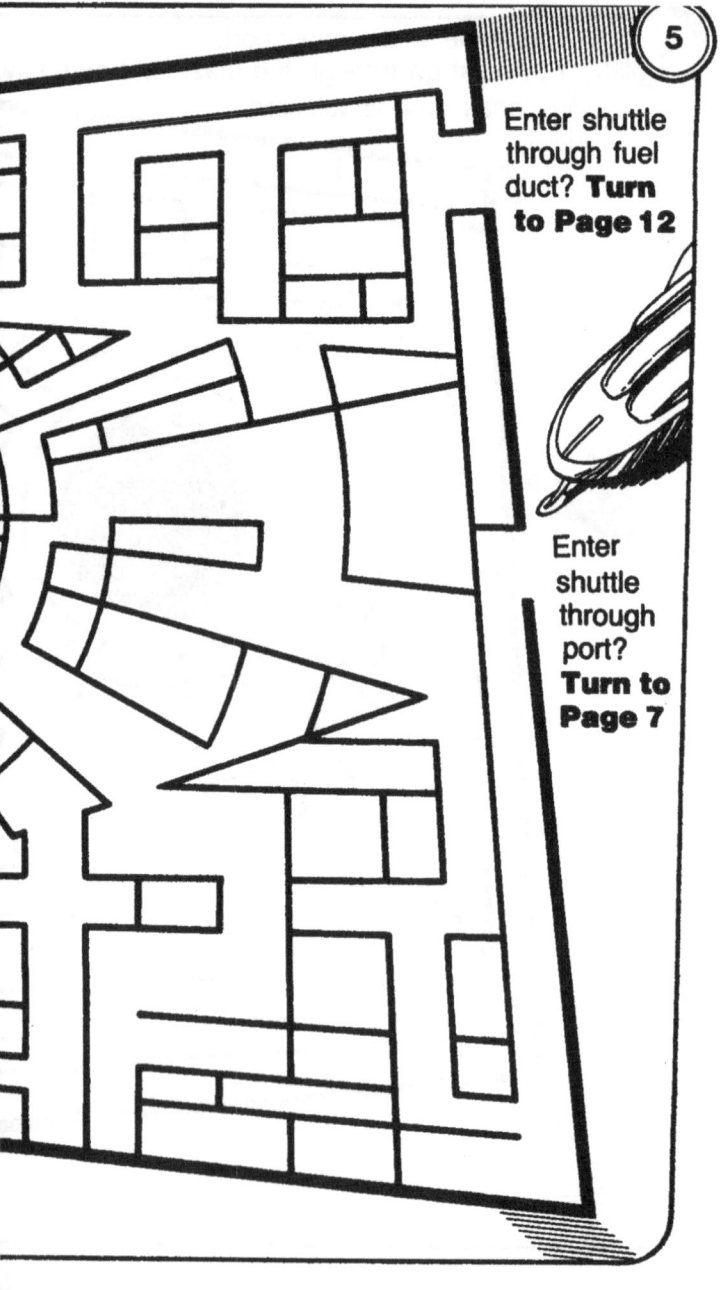

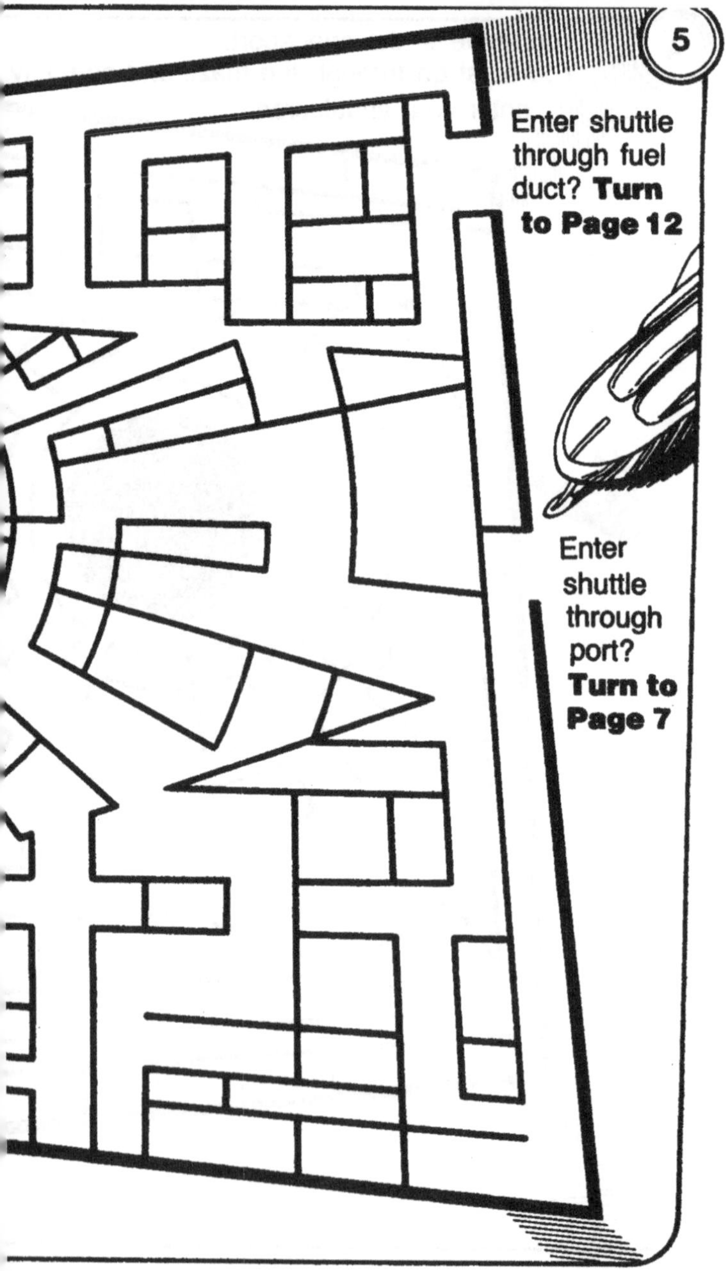

Enter shuttle through fuel duct? **Turn to Page 12**

Enter shuttle through port? **Turn to Page 7**

You are ready to set your course. Phatax's movements have been monitored by Interplanetary Spy Tracking Stations.

To find out which space sector he is in now, count the number of *broken* circles below. Each circle represents one space sector.

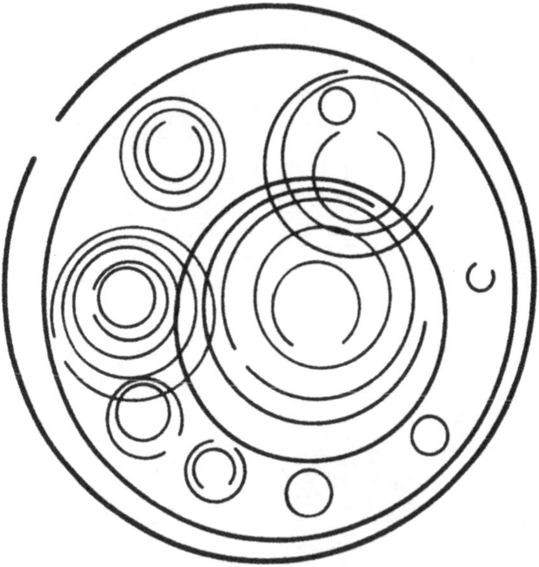

13 broken circles? Turn to Page 13

14 broken circles? Turn to Page 60

Another number? Turn to Page 121

Good! You are now in the shuttle.
You are ready for more data on Phatax:

When Phatax kidnapped Prince Quizon, he stole the Royal Jewels, which have special powers. You must get the prince *and* the jewels back!

These are Phatax's disguises:

This is his starcruiser:

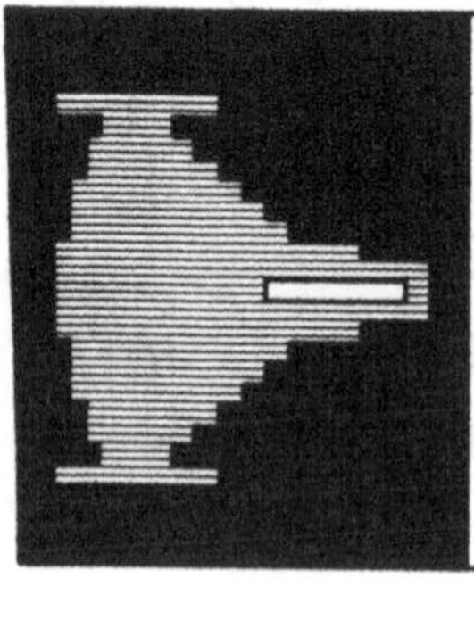

These are the Royal Jewels:

Turn to Page 8

16
This is the correct firing order:
Three. . . Two. . . One. . .
BLAST

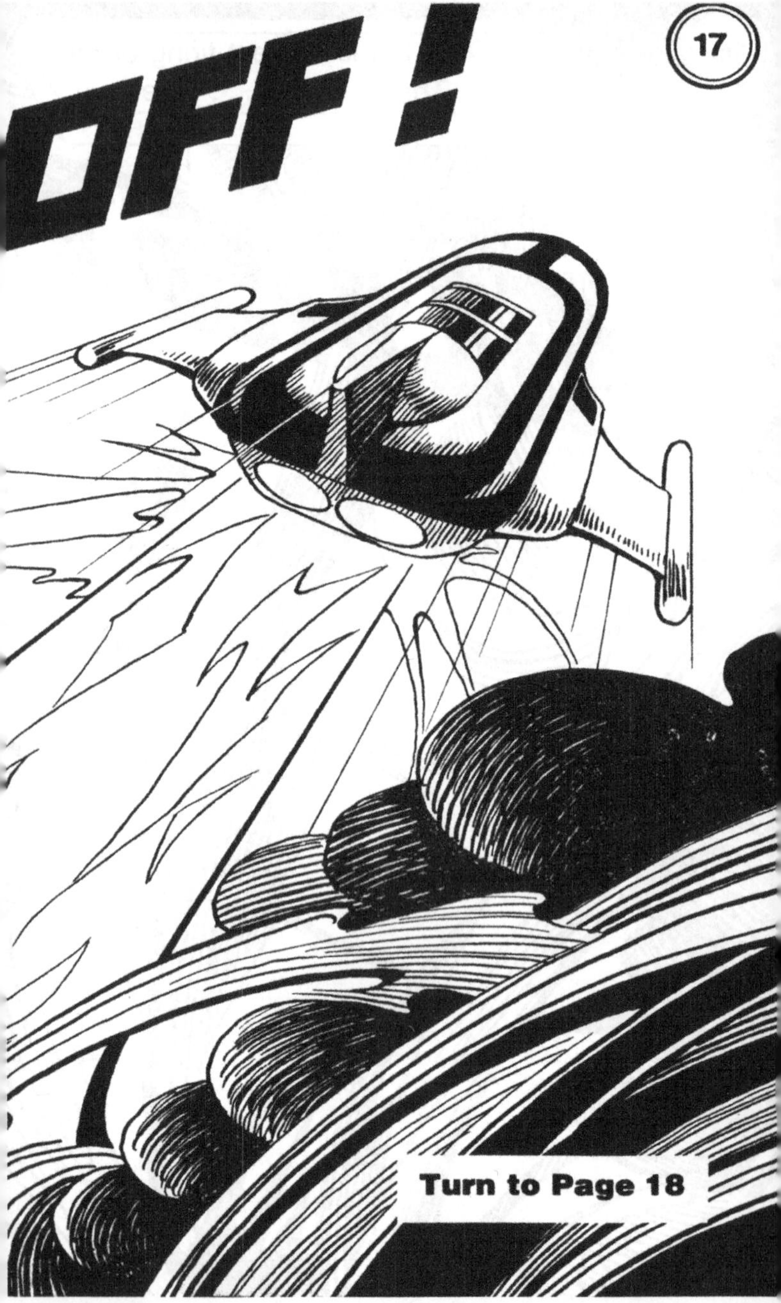

Turn to Page 18

18

You are on your way to the planet Threefax!

Enter the following personal data, so that the computer can match it with what is known about Phatax:

Your Height ☐' ☐☐"

Your Weight ☐☐☐ **lbs.**

Your code name for this mission will be:

S	T	A	R	S	C	A	N

Warning! Warning! Warning!

Turn to Page 31

You fire on it and miss!

Now your viewscreen shows that the object is a meteor coming right at you!

To hit it, you must program your missile to fly through the maze of drifting rocks.

Turn to Page 25

As your ship travels through space, you approach an unknown object hidden by swirling gas and asteroids.

If you want to fire at this object before it gets any closer, turn to Page 19

If you want to approach this object to see what it is, turn to Page 22

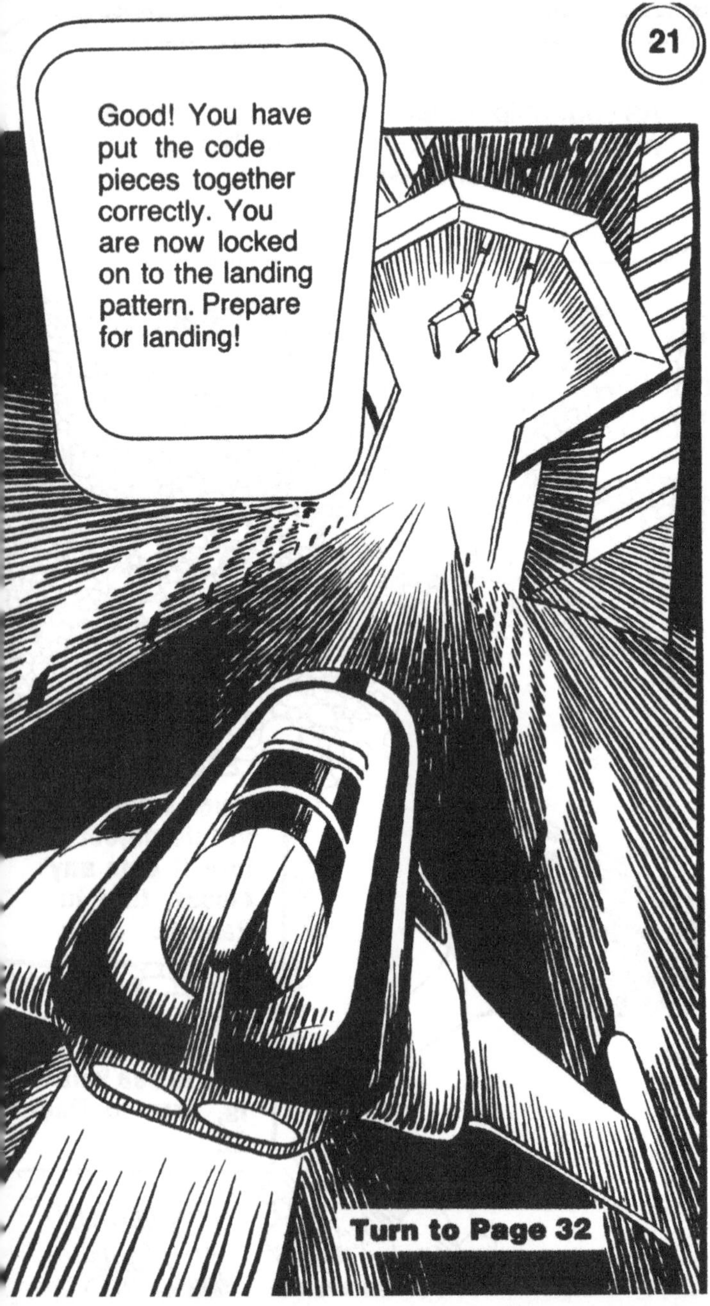
Good! You have put the code pieces together correctly. You are now locked on to the landing pattern. Prepare for landing!
Turn to Page 32

22

As you approach the object, sensor readout identifies it as a meteor, containing Mendelum 87-A. Mendelum can be used as fuel for your starship.

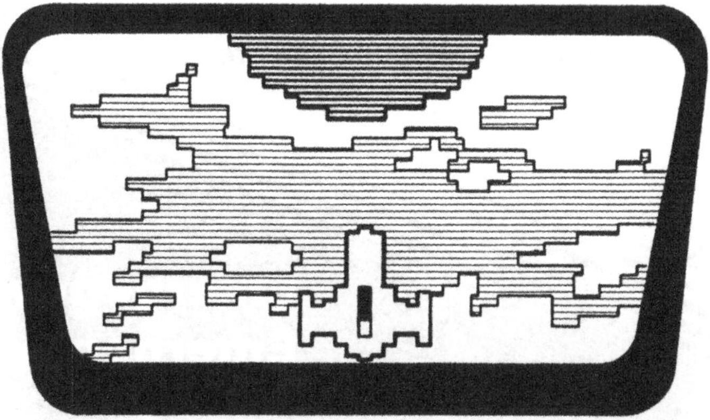

To get to the meteor and the Mendelum, guide your ship through the maze of asteroids.

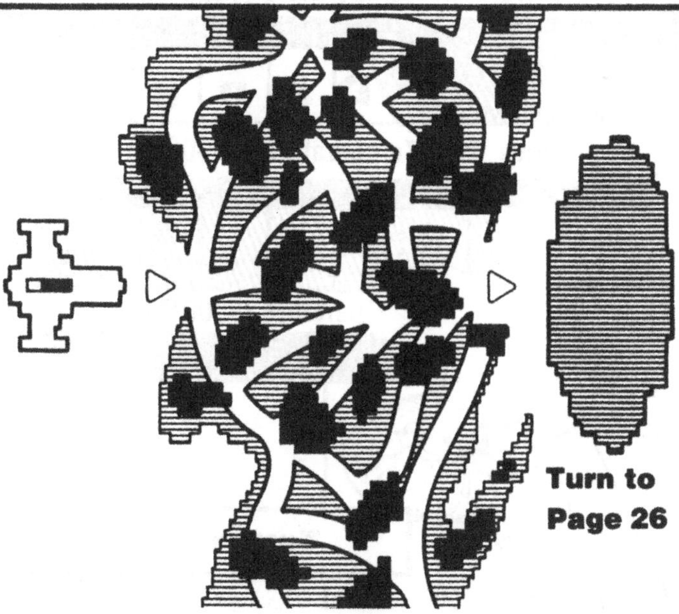

Turn to Page 26

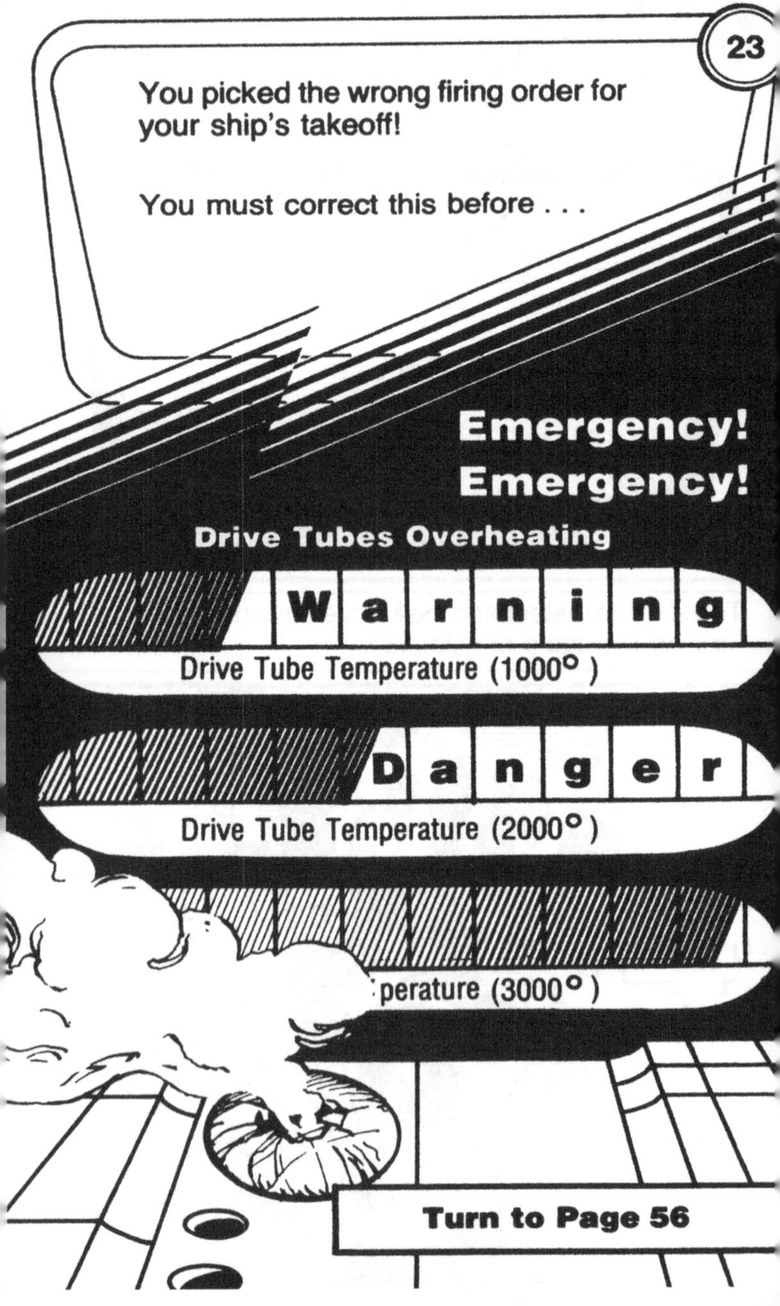
You picked the wrong firing order for your ship's takeoff!
You must correct this before . . .
Emergency!
Emergency!
Drive Tubes Overheating
Warning
Drive Tube Temperature (1000°)
Danger
Drive Tube Temperature (2000°)
perature (3000°)

Turn to Page 56

Suddenly, a monstrous figure beams in behind you. He has a blaster out and he tells you to freeze!
He is one of Phatax's agents! You cannot escape! **Turn to Page 35**

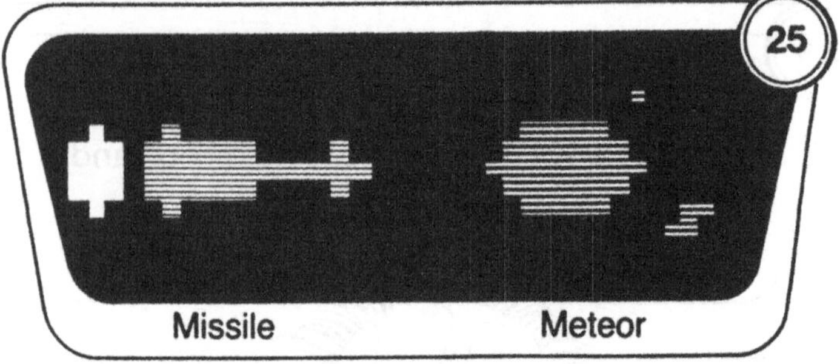

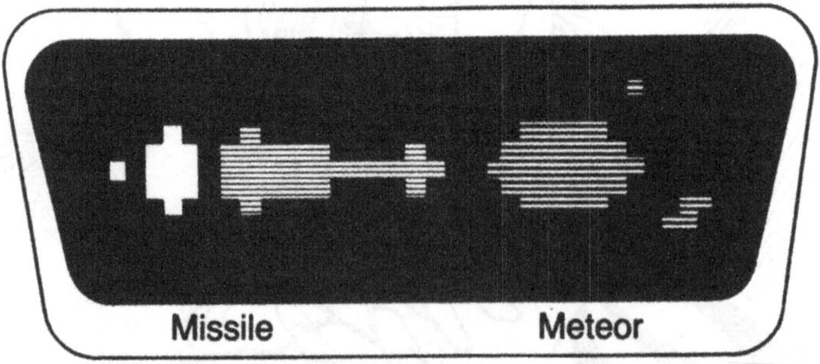

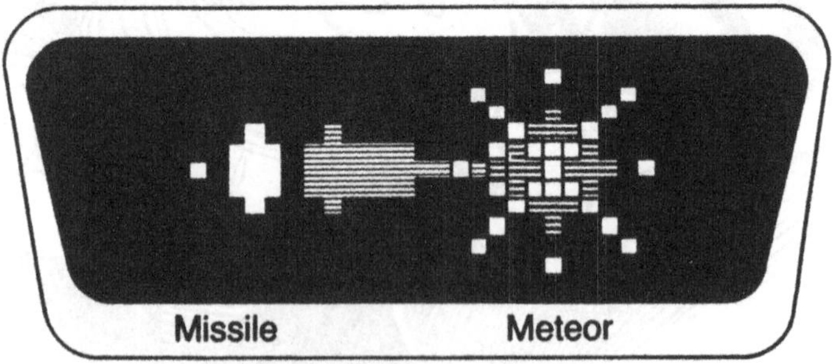

Damage!

The meteor explosion has damaged your ship. Your engines are dead. You will drift through space. . . forever!

26
You use the meteor to make extra fuel. Then you head for Threefax at superspeed.
As you approach the planet, the computer tells you to send a message to Tavro, the Interplanetary Spy on Threefax. Tavro is in Barenga, the capital city.
You send a message to Tavro by laser, telling him to contact you after you land.
Next you call the Barenga spaceport and request permission to land.
Turn to Page 27

Stand by to receive message from Spaceport Control Tower.

Greetings! Permission granted to land at Barenga Spaceport. Stand by for coded landing instructions.

Instructions being sent to computer for decoding:

Transmission complete. To lock on to landing pattern, turn to Page 28.

28

After your computer decodes the landing instructions from the spaceport, this shape appears on your screen:

To land your ship, you must duplicate this landing pattern shape. Using the code pieces shown below, form the landing pattern shape.

A B C D E F

You can use a piece more than once.

Turn to the next page

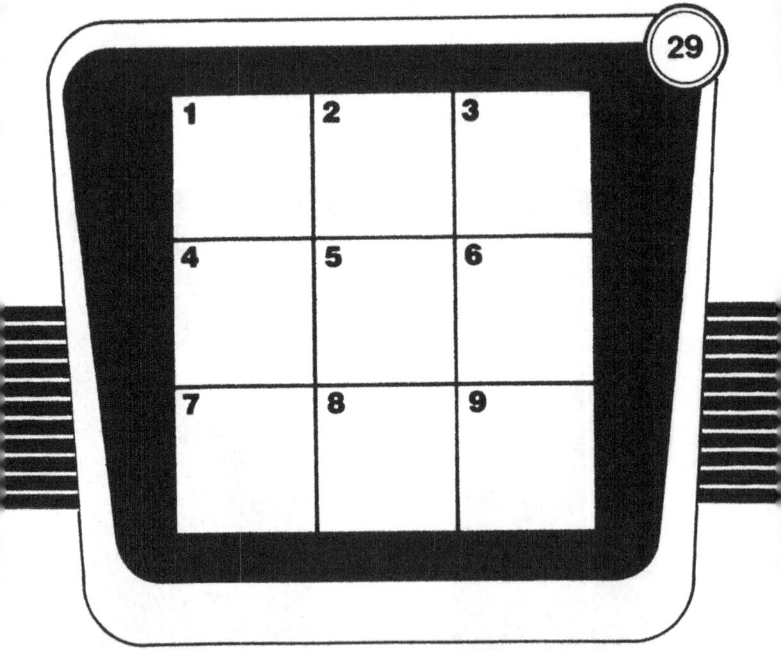

Enter the letters which stand for the code pieces. Put them in the correct order to form the landing pattern.

Repeat the letters below. Follow the number order above.

1	2	3	4	5	6	7	8	9

Your computer gives you three likely patterns.

If you choose: C D A E F C D D E
turn to Page 30

If you choose: C D B E C F A C B
turn to Page 121

If you choose: C B D E B F A B A
turn to Page 21

30
You picked the wrong landing pattern! The Threefaxians
decide you must be an en-
emy spy. They blast you!
The End

The computer reveals a dangerous difference between your size and that of Phatax:

Compared to you, Phatax is a giant!
Phatax, like all Kirillians, is at least 15 times larger than a human.
Starscan
Phatax

To protect yourself on Threefax, these defensive weapons may be helpful. You may wear one or both.

☐ Take: Stun-gas belt (each charge can stun a large animal)

☐ Take: Snare ring (can trap and stun any creature)

Turn to Page 20

Red Alert! Your ship is too small for the landing grapplers. Most of the ships that land in Barenga belong to giants.

You must increase the size your ship to fit the giant landir grappler

Turn to Page 3

Computer photo shows the current sizes of your ship and the landing grapplers.

How many times larger should you make your ship to fit the landing grapplers?

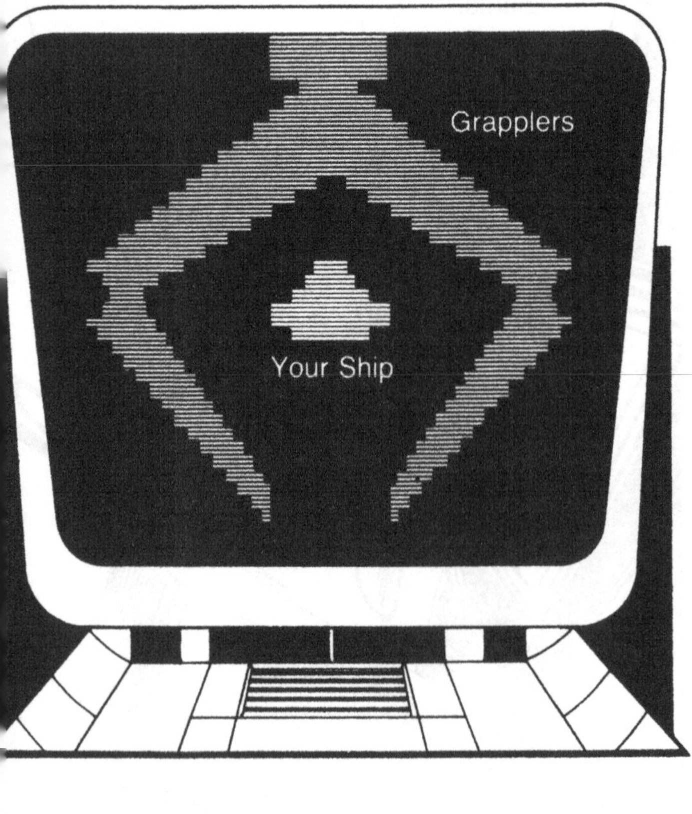

Increase ship size three times? Turn to Page 34

Increase ship size six times? Turn to Page 56

The control tower warns you: If you make an error, your ship may crash into the grapplers and blow up!

Good. Your ship expands by molecular duplication.

Ship size: Number of expansions

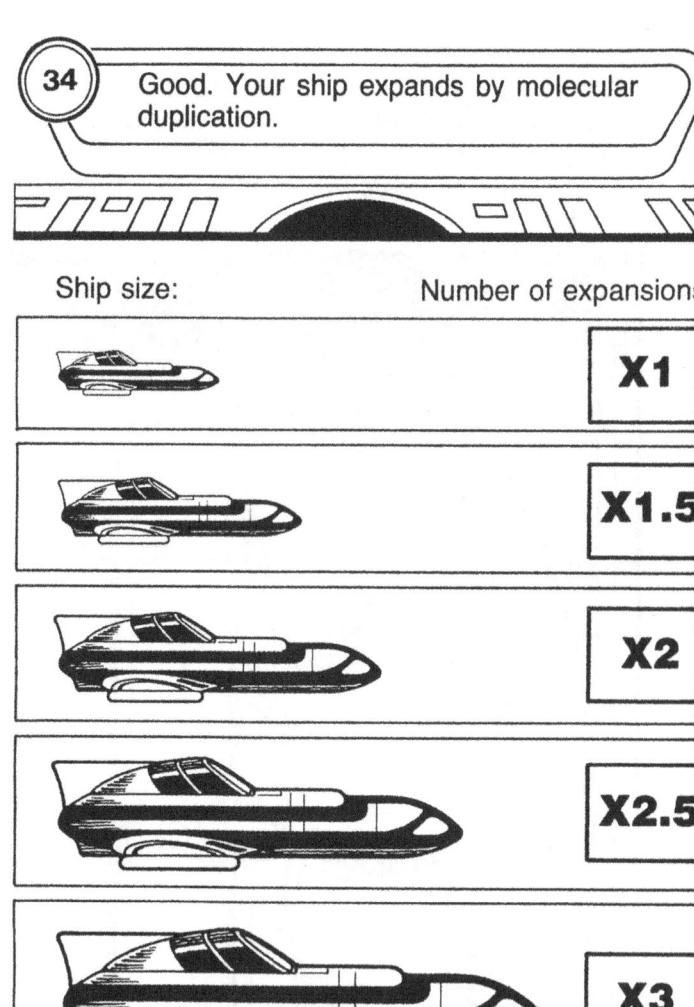

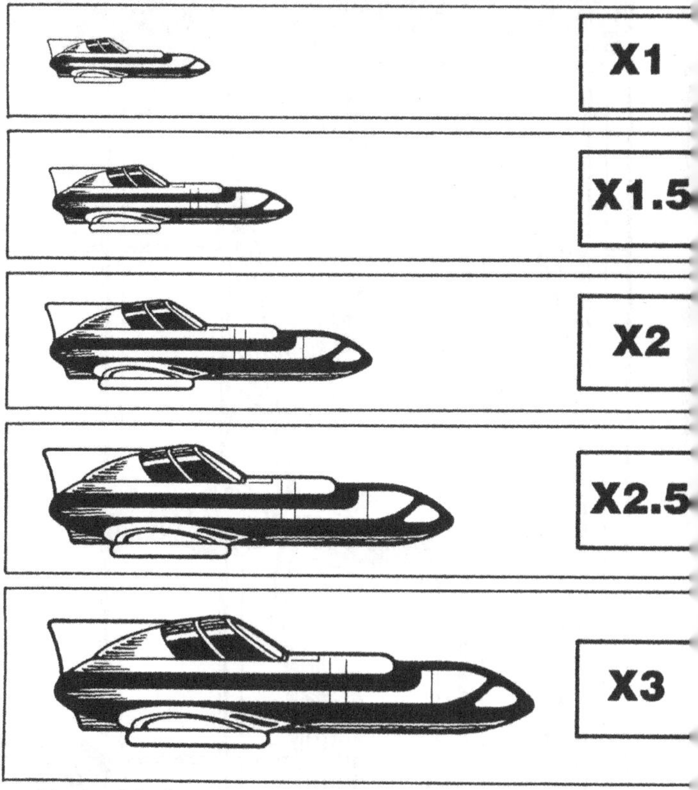

Your ship is now the correct size for the grapplers.

Turn to Page 41

Phatax's agent fires a paralyzing ray at you. You pass out. When you wake up, you are in a dungeon on the planet Kirillia. It may be years before you can escape.

36
Tavro, the Interplanetary Spy on the planet Threefax, has left a pouch for Starscan, your code name! You get it. In it is a message and half of a medallion. You decode the message: *Meet me today at 16:00 at Barenga Park. Phatax's agents and robot dogs are on my trail. Be careful!*
You reduce the size of your ship and leave. You must meet Tavro in two hours!
16:00
-2:00
Turn to Page 37

You leave gate 42 of the spaceport and make your way toward the city. Your size makes it easy to hide. Barenga is a city of giants! Going by foot takes you longer than you expected, but it is the best way to avoid Phatax's agents. You know nothing about Tavro except that he is human-size and a mutant.
Turn to Page 38

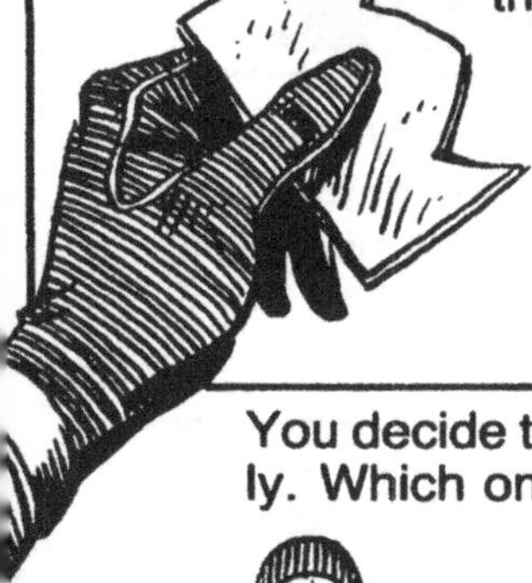

You come to Barenga Park at last. You see three statues. Something about them is familiar! You look at the medallion that Tavro sent you.

Similar medallions hang from the neck of each statue. One of them might fit yours.

You decide to look at the statues more closely. Which one do you check out first?

Kapar? Turn to Page 49

Savamp? Turn to Page 121

Orvat? Turn to Page 74

BEEP! BEEP! BEEP!

Collision Alarm Activated

You fly through the Royal Palace. Suddenly your computer warns you of a dangerous animal in your flight path. Part of the animal flashes on the viewscreen. There is no time to see the rest. You must act now to avoid a crash!

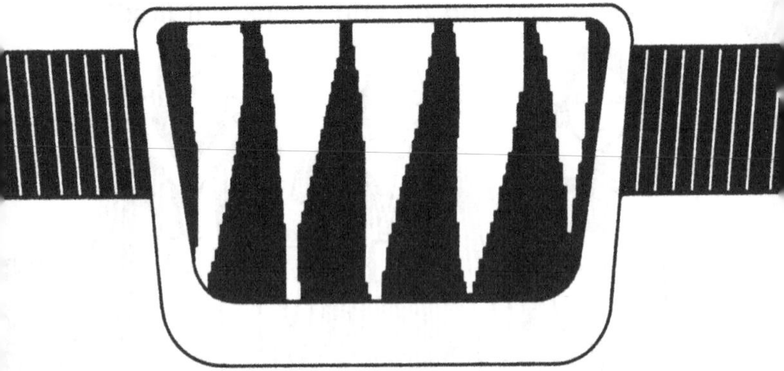

If the animal is an Octopod, you must fly ***above*** its back to avoid deadly tentacles. If it is a Megaron, you must fly ***below*** its belly to avoid the spikes on its back. Is it a Megaron or an Octopod on the viewscreen above? Quick!

Megaron? Turn to Page 45

Octopod? Turn to Page 50

You ride the robot dog to your ship, but you decide not to keep it. Phatax may have programmed it to blow up. You let it go.

You are now ready to search for Prince Quizon. He is hidden somewhere in the Royal Palace. Tavro gave you information that should help you to find it. Your ship blasts off for the center of Barenga.

Turn to Page 42

You approach the grapplers again.

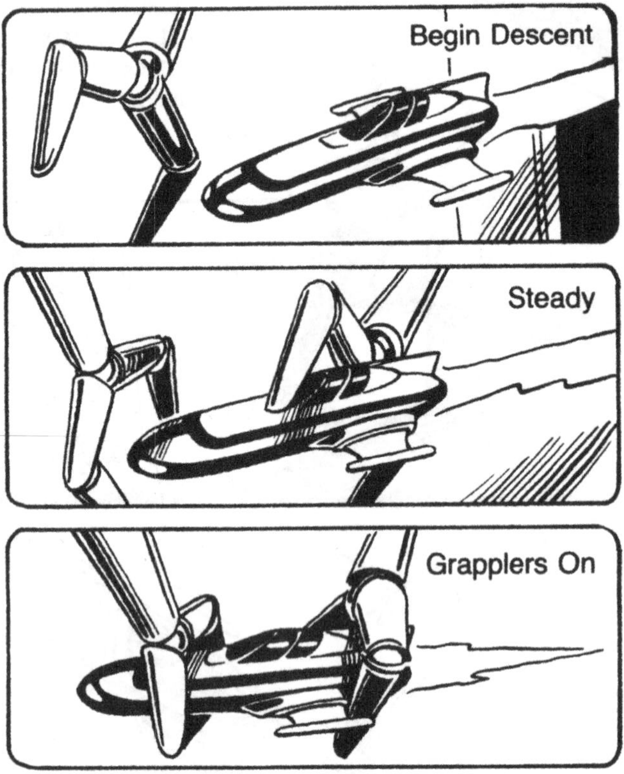
Begin Descent
Steady
Grapplers On

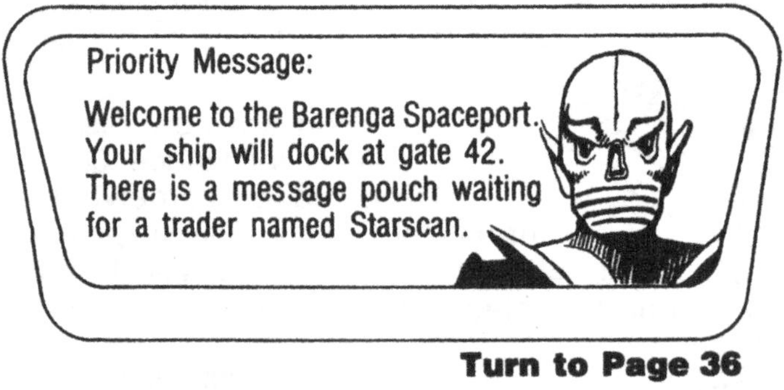
Priority Message:
Welcome to the Barenga Spaceport.
Your ship will dock at gate 42.
There is a message pouch waiting
for a trader named Starscan.

Turn to Page 36

You reach the center of Barenga.
You are looking for the Royal Palace.

Scanner magnification: normal
Distance: 100 kad-miles

Scanner magnification: normal
Distance: 50 kad-miles

Turn to Page 43

Scanner magnification: normal
Distance: 2 kad-miles

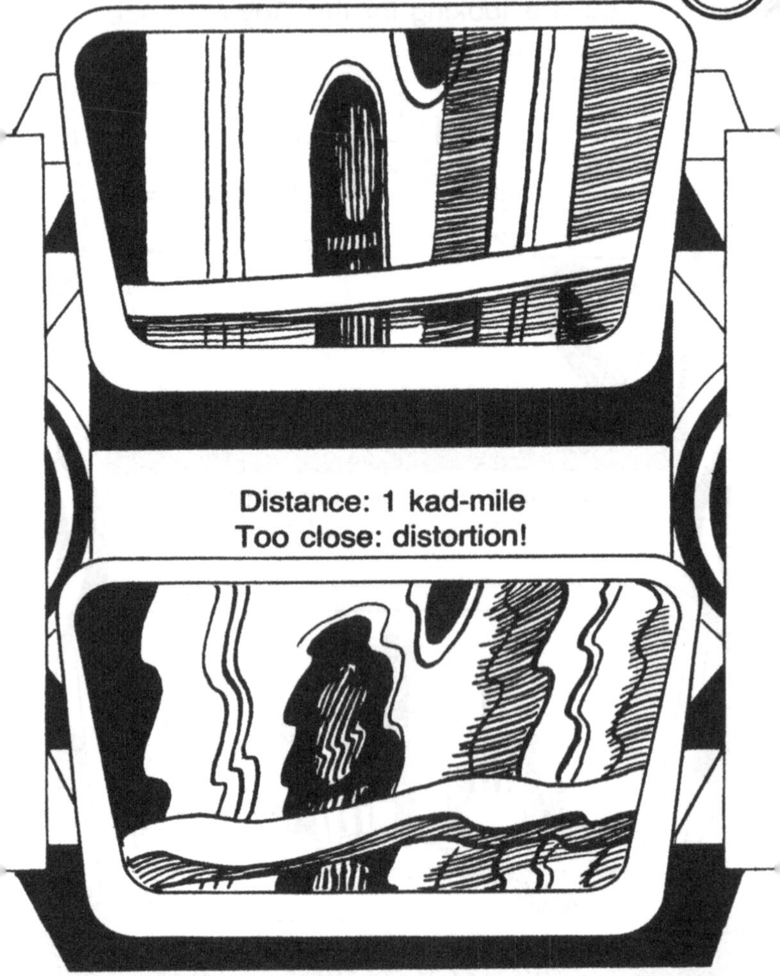

Danger! This close, the buildings are so big that the scanner cannot see more than part of any single building. Slow down to navigate!

Turn to Page 44

44

You are moving so fast, and you are so close, that your scanner cannot see the whole picture! You take close-up scan pictures:

Scan 1 Scan 2 Scan 3

You can compare the close-up scans to a picture of the Royal Palace that Tavro gave you.

Which of the three close-up scans shows a part of the Royal Palace? Look at Tavro's picture and choose. Then proceed there immediately.

Scan 1? Turn to Page 51
Scan 2? Turn to Page 46
Scan 3? Turn to Page 55

It is a Megaron! You dive under the Megaron's belly, avoiding the dangerous spikes on its back. You resume your search for Prince Quizon.

You must be careful. Phatax and his agents could be anywhere in the Royal Palace.

Turn to Page 47

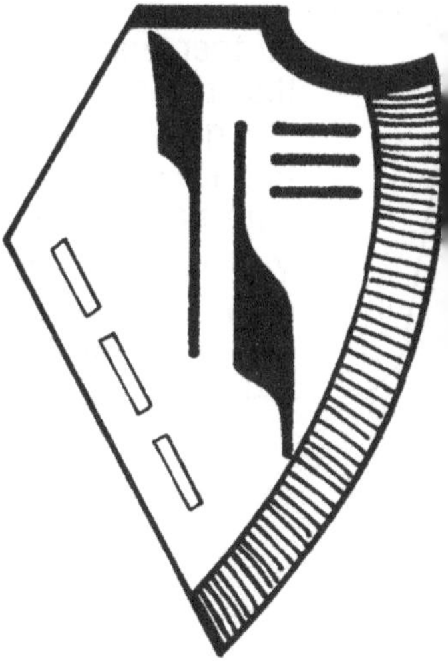

You fly closer to the building shown in Scan 2. It looks like a palace, but you are not sure. Tavro gave you a picture of the Royal Crest. He said the crest would be part of the decoration on the palace walls.

You fly past the building. Is the Royal Crest there?

Turn to Page 48

Further inside, your computer tells you that the palace has hundreds of rooms. The quickest way to find Prince Quizon is to track his voice. But first you must make sure he is inside.

You have Prince Quizon's voiceprint in your computer. You use the computer to search for the sound of the prince's voice.

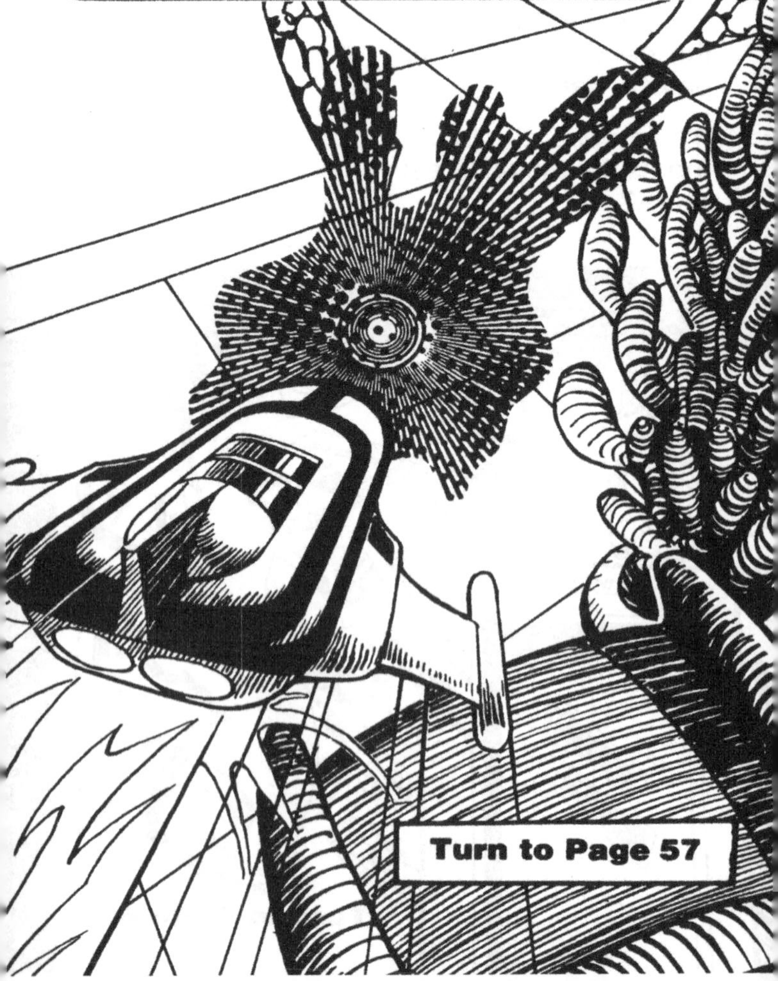

Turn to Page 57

48

You find the Royal Crest! You circle the palace to find a way inside. But all the entrances are guarded by giants.

You locate a keyhole in one of the palace doors. Your ship is just small enough to fly through it.

Turn to Page 39

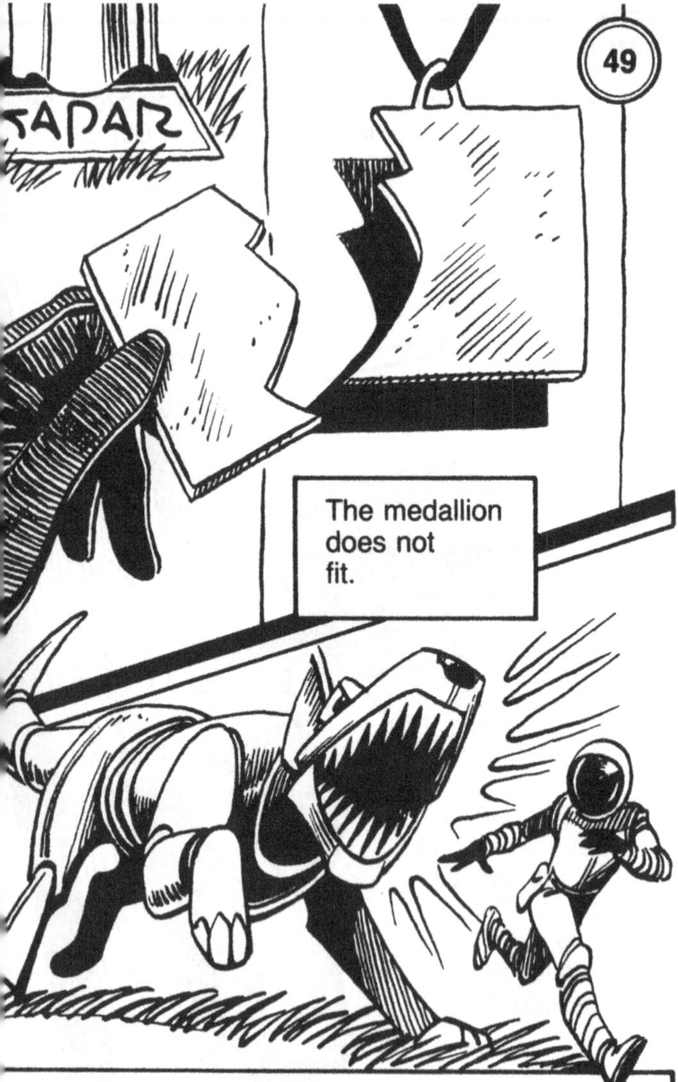
The medallion does not fit.

efore you can check one of the the other statues, you ear a loud barking. It is one of Phatax's deadly robot gs. Run!

Turn to Page 54

50

You fly your ship higher to avoid the Octopod's tentacles. But suddenly you see spikes in front of you. Octopods do not have spikes! You are flying into the spikes of a Megaron!

You fly toward the building shown in Scan 1. As you get closer, your ship is sucked into a giant whirling vent. Your ship is being drawn into the:

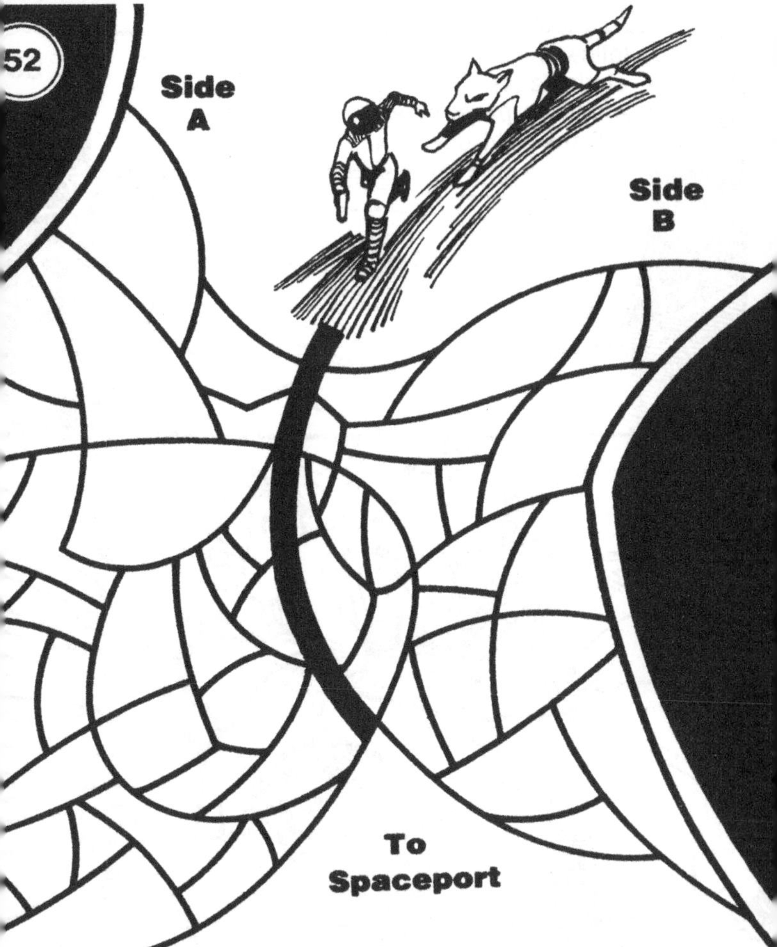

The robot dog chases you. You are cornered at the front wall of a stone barrier!
You can blast your way to the safety of the spaceport on the other side. But you only have six shots to do it! One shot will knock down one wall of the barrier. Which side of the barrier can you escape through with only six blasts?

A? Turn to Page 54 **B? Turn to Page 59**

You follow the sound that generated voiceprint B. The static fades. Your computer picks up the prince's voice pattern clearly. You know you are going in the right direction.

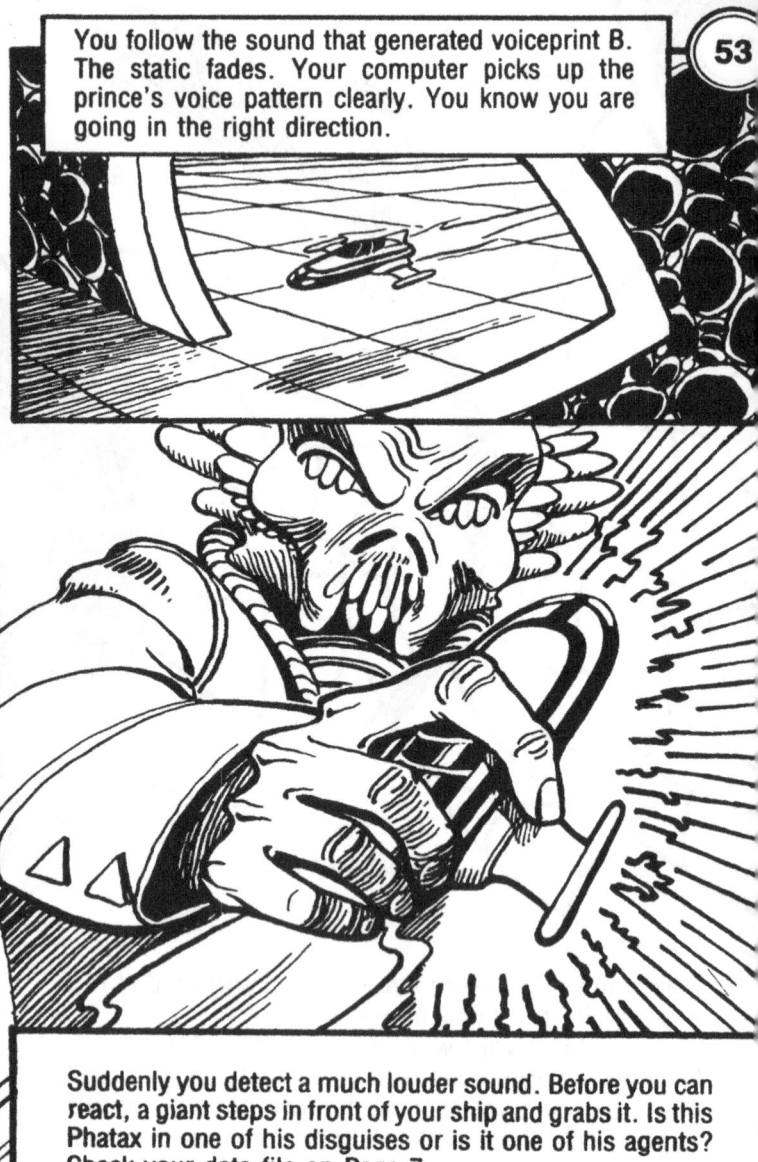

Suddenly you detect a much louder sound. Before you can react, a giant steps in front of your ship and grabs it. Is this Phatax in one of his disguises or is it one of his agents? Check your data file on Page 7.

Turn to Page 61

54
The End
The robot dog traps you against a wall. You cannot escape!

You fly toward the building shown in Scan 3. Your view is blocked by clouds of mist! You try to reverse your flight pattern, but you are drawn into the heart of the:
Barenga Vaporization Plant
The End

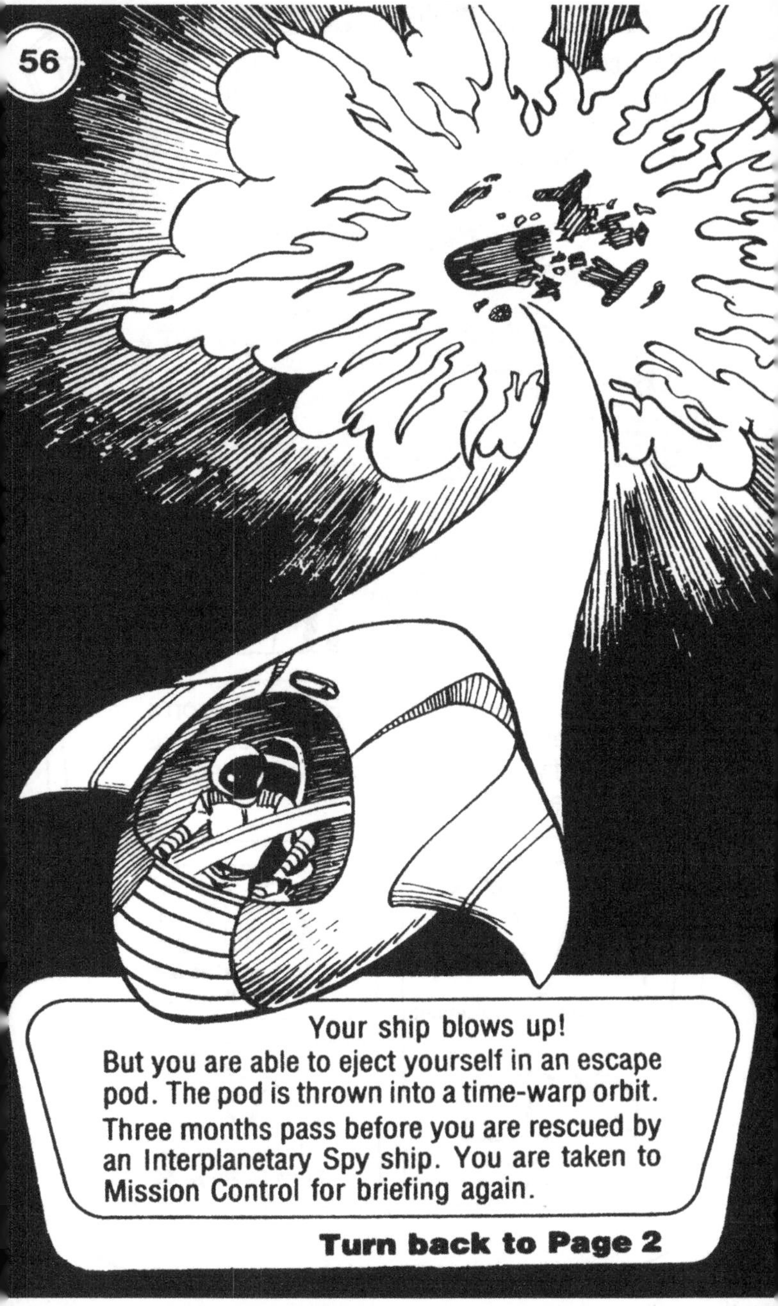

Your ship blows up!

But you are able to eject yourself in an escape pod. The pod is thrown into a time-warp orbit. Three months pass before you are rescued by an Interplanetary Spy ship. You are taken to Mission Control for briefing again.

Turn back to Page 2

Your computer picks up two similar voiceprints and a lot of static. You are sure one of the prints matches Prince Quizon's, but it is hard to tell since the computer blends the static with the voiceprints.

Which voiceprint has Prince Quizon's voiceprint hidden in it? Choose one and fly in the direction that the sound comes from.

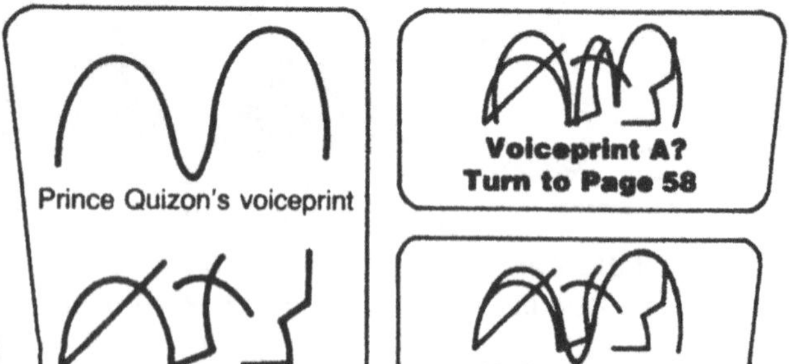
Prince Quizon's voiceprint
Static pattern, with no voice
Voiceprint A? Turn to Page 58
Voiceprint B? Turn to Page 53

58
You fly in the direction of the sound that generated voiceprint A.

But it does not lead you to Prince Quizon. Instead, it leads you straight into the hands of a Genrax! Threefaxians keep Genraxes for pets. And the Genrax is going to keep YOU for a pet . . .until it gets hungry.
The End

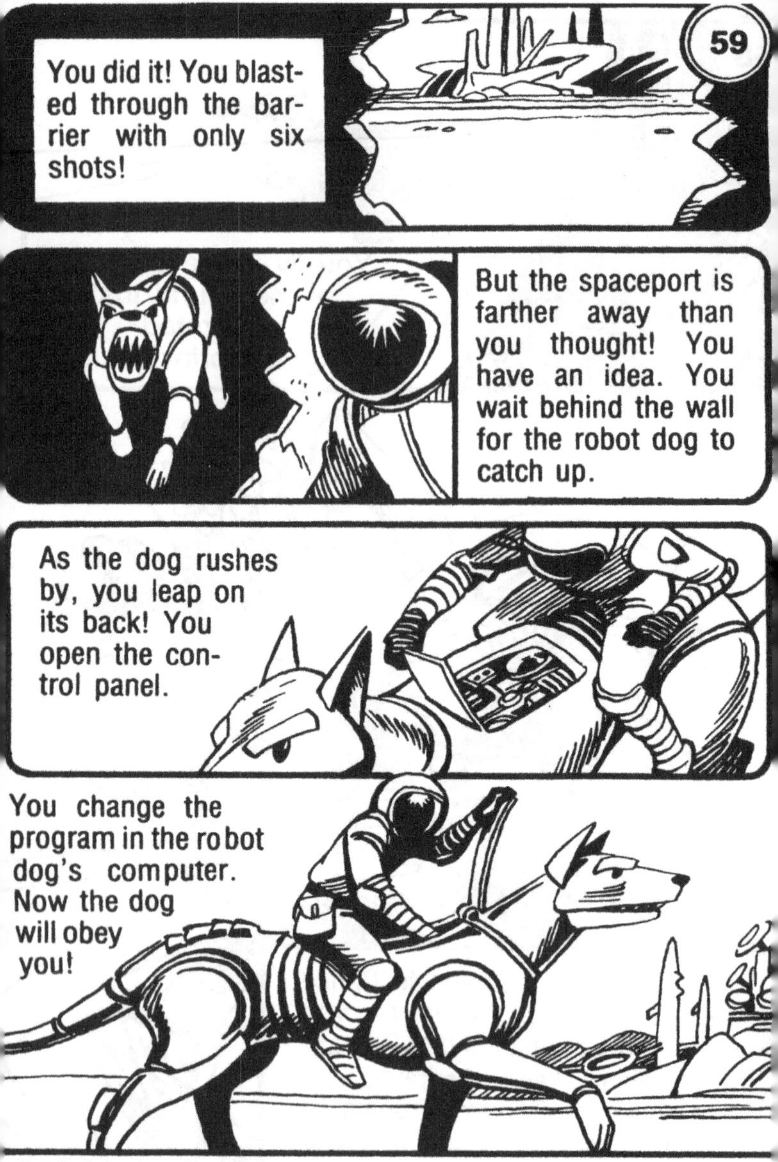
You did it! You blasted through the barrier with only six shots!
But the spaceport is farther away than you thought! You have an idea. You wait behind the wall for the robot dog to catch up.
As the dog rushes by, you leap on its back! You open the control panel.
You change the program in the robot dog's computer. Now the dog will obey you!

You order the robot dog to take you to the spaceport.

Turn to Page 40

60

Your ship takes off automatically. You head toward Sector 14. Your computer warns you that this is an uncharted sector of space. You realize you have made a mistake! Perhaps you can get back by taking a shortcut.

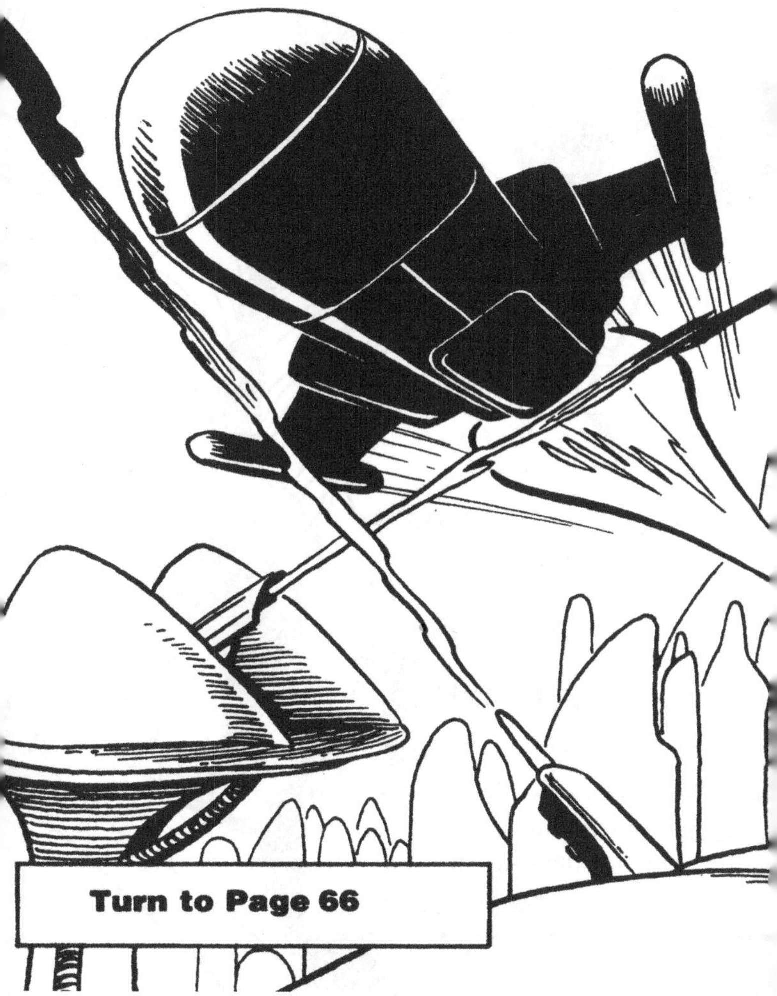

Turn to Page 66

You realize that the giant's face is *not* one of Phatax's disguises. But this giant is still dangerous. He opens the hatch of the ship!

Before he can pull you out, you fire your jet pack to escape.

Turn to Page 75

"You are too late," Prince Quizon exclaims. "Phatax has taken the Royal Jewels to be sold!"

You question the prince, but he is so upset he cannot remember anything else Phatax said.

You must do a mind probe. The prince may have overheard something that will tell you where Phatax went. You can use the tattoo on Prince Quizon's forehead to focus your probe.

Concentrate on the dot in the center of the mind-probe pattern above for one minute. Then look at the tattoo on Prince Quizon's forehead on the next page. What do you see?

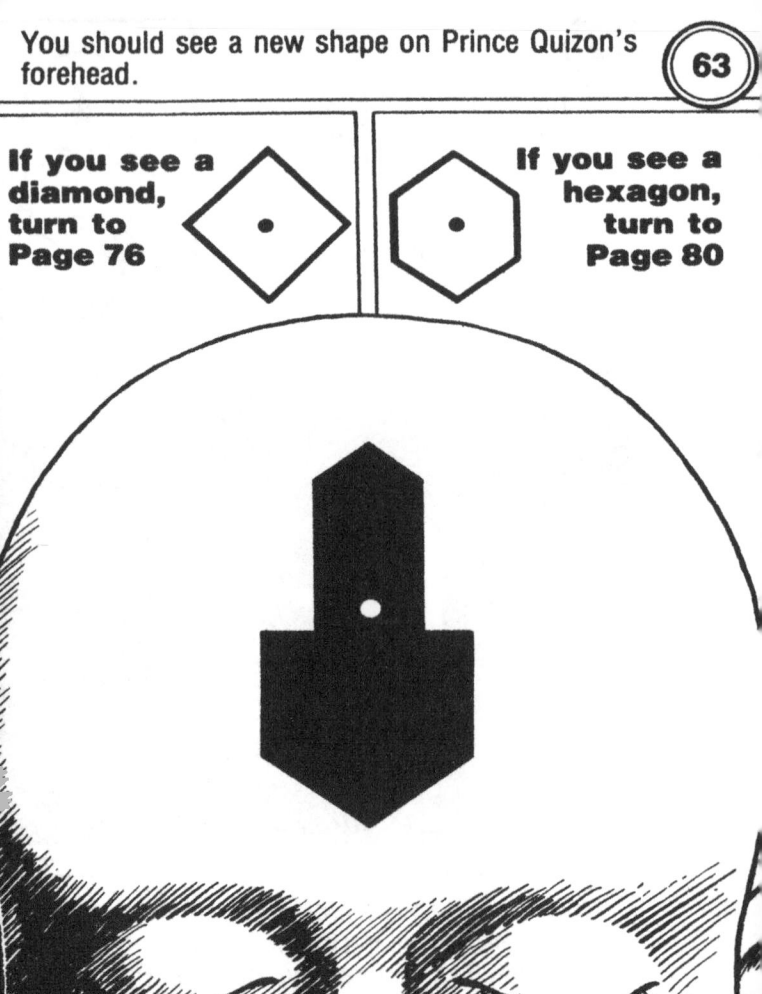

If you see a diamond, turn to Page 76

If you see a hexagon, turn to Page 80

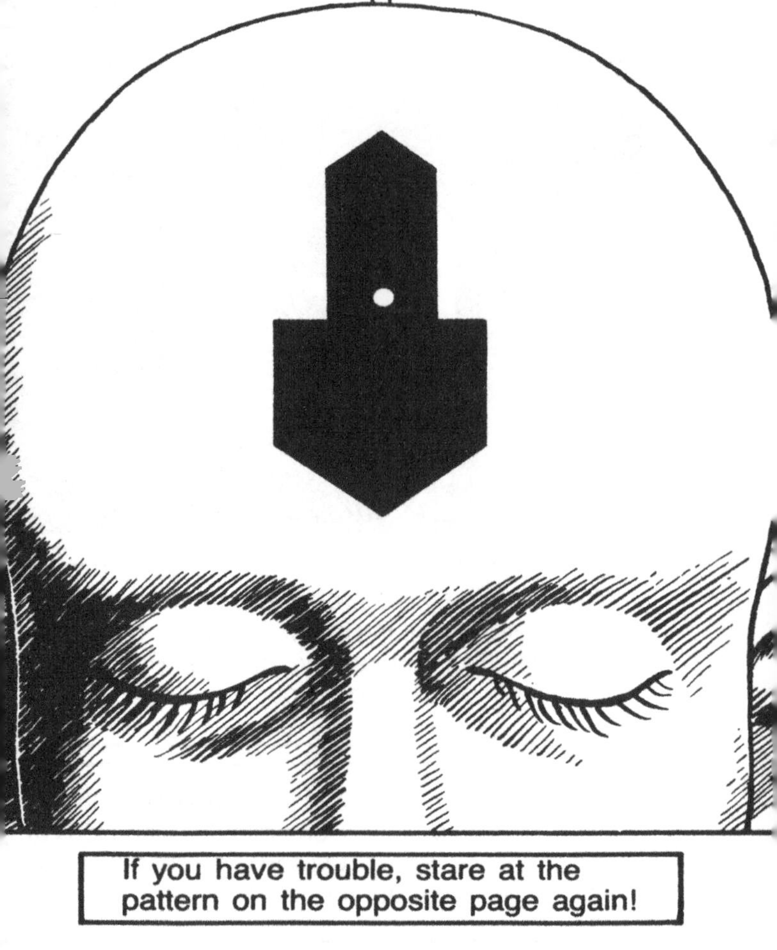

If you have trouble, stare at the pattern on the opposite page again!

You take out the snare ring! You must choose the right shape to snare the giant by his ankle.

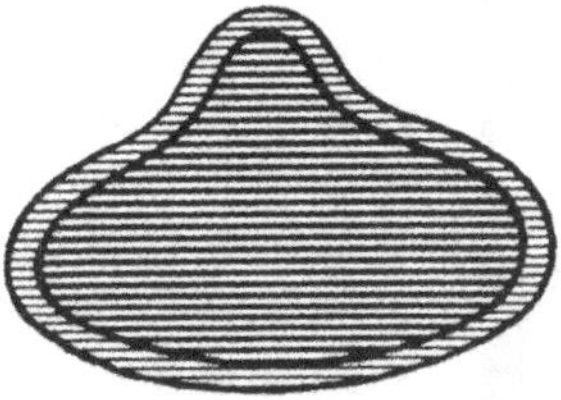

You study the giant's ankle from all sides. It has this shape when seen from above.

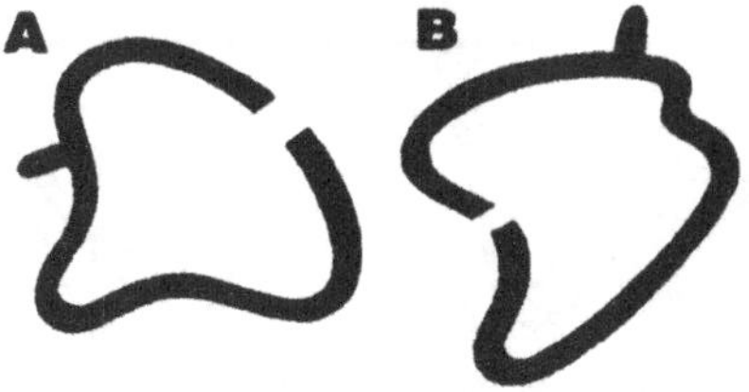

Pick one of the snare ring's two shapes. Only one shape will fit the giant's ankle. If you can snare him, the stun ray from the ring will make him pass out.

Pattern A? Turn to Page 71

Pattern B? Turn to Page 24

Too bad! You didn't fold your wings enough. Your ship is still too wide to fit between the strings.
The child smashes your ship with his racket! Your ship crashes through a palace window.
You are a victim of Interplanetary Tennis!
The End

66

As you cross the uncharted space of Sector 14, a warning flashes from your computer screen:

WARNING! WARNING! SHIP NOW HEADED TOWARD A BLACK HOLE.

There is no escape as your starship is pulled into the black hole.

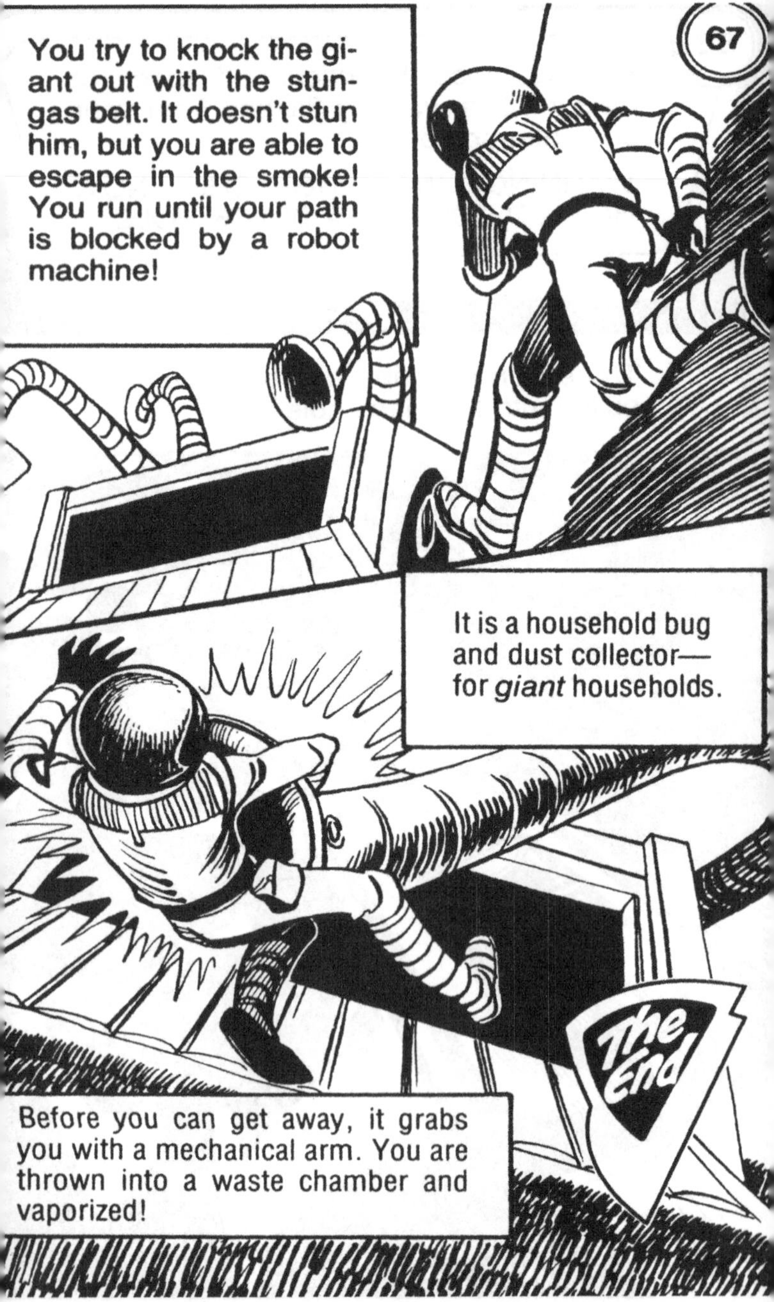
You try to knock the giant out with the stun-gas belt. It doesn't stun him, but you are able to escape in the smoke! You run until your path is blocked by a robot machine!
It is a household bug and dust collector—for *giant* households.
Before you can get away, it grabs you with a mechanical arm. You are thrown into a waste chamber and vaporized!
The End

You fly your ship through the palace sculptures.
You follow Prince Quizon's voice-print, but as you do, you pick up a fast-moving object on your screen.
Suddenly, you see spaceship comi toward you! It is t same size as yo ship.
SENSOR READOUT: Approaching *ship does* not contain living beings.

Turn to Page 6

The uninhabited ship is plucked out of the air by a giant alien child. The ship is his toy!

Now he looks at you. He must think that your ship is one of his toys. He's going to swat you with his racket!

Turn to Page 70

You can escape by flying between the rac
strings. You must make your ship smaller!

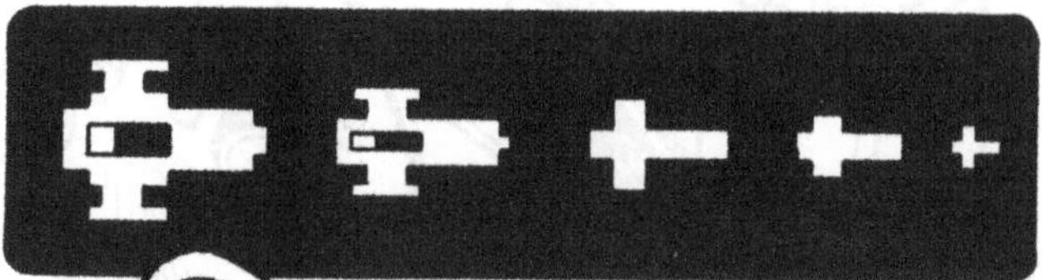

Your ship is too wide. You must fold your ship's wings. But if you don't fold them enough, you will fly right into the racket strings.

FOLD SHIP'S WINGS TO ANGLE:

60 DEGREES

PRESS HERE
then turn to Page 72

30 DEGREES

PRESS HERE
then turn to Page 65

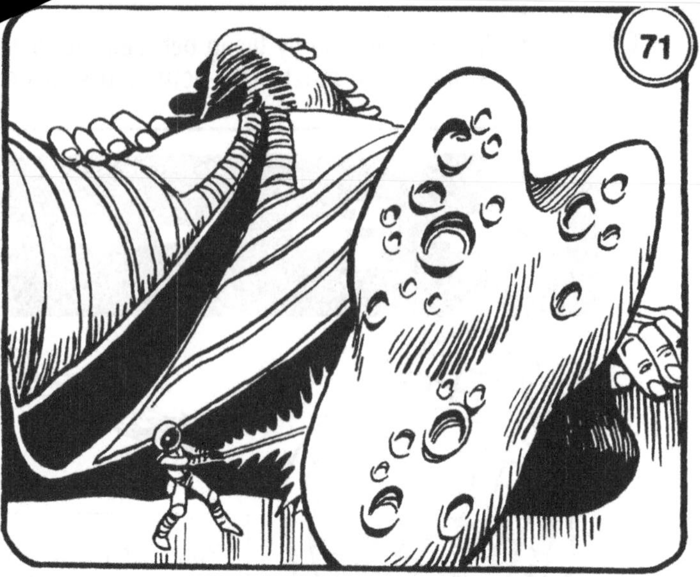

The snare ring works! The giant passes out from the ring's stun ray. You rush back to your ship.
Prince Quizon's voiceprint is changing shape. Your computer tells you that it may be a call from the prince, in deep distress.

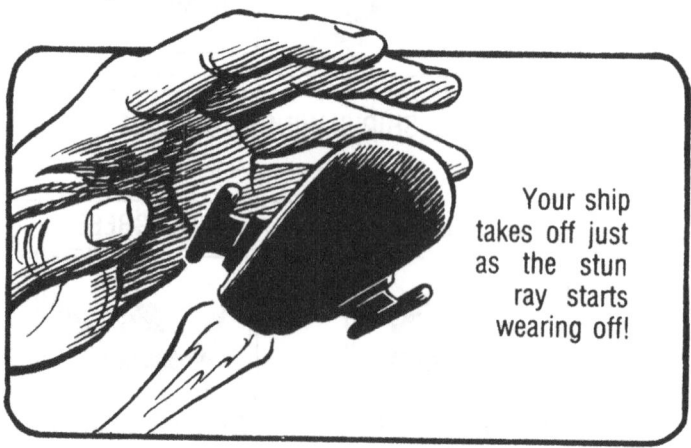

Your ship takes off just as the stun ray starts wearing off!

Turn to Page 68

Good! You pass through the holes in the racket easily and escape the child.

You can now see Prince Quizon's voiceprint clearly. You are getting closer!

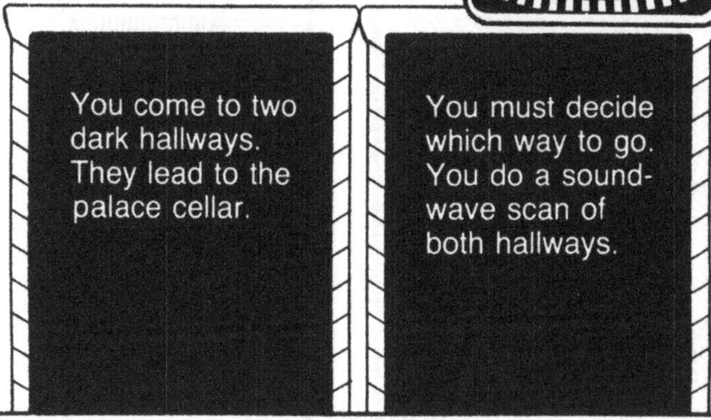

You come to two dark hallways. They lead to the palace cellar.
You must decide which way to go. You do a sound-wave scan of both hallways.

By using your sound-wave scan, you determine that one hallway leads to a multidimensional transport chamber.

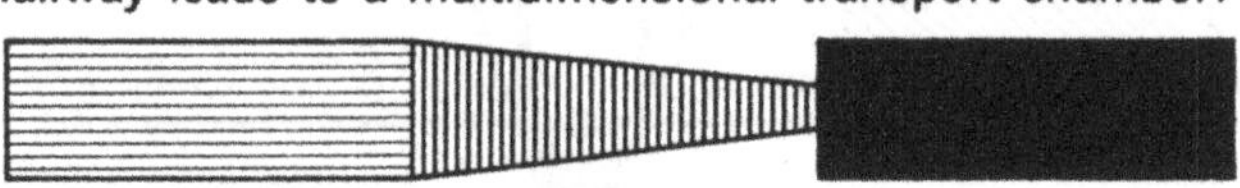

The other hallway leads toward a chamber that holds Prince Quizon!

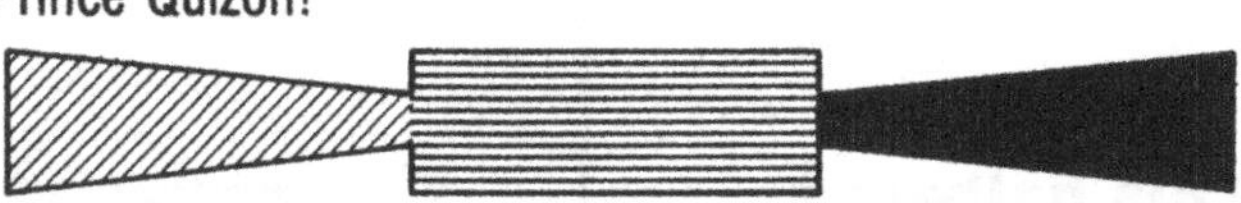

Turn to Page 73

But the sound-wave scan only shows you a flat picture of each hallway. You must decide which sound-wave scan comes from which hallway. Choose the hallway that leads to the prince!

Hurry! You don't have much time. The giant guard is on your trail!

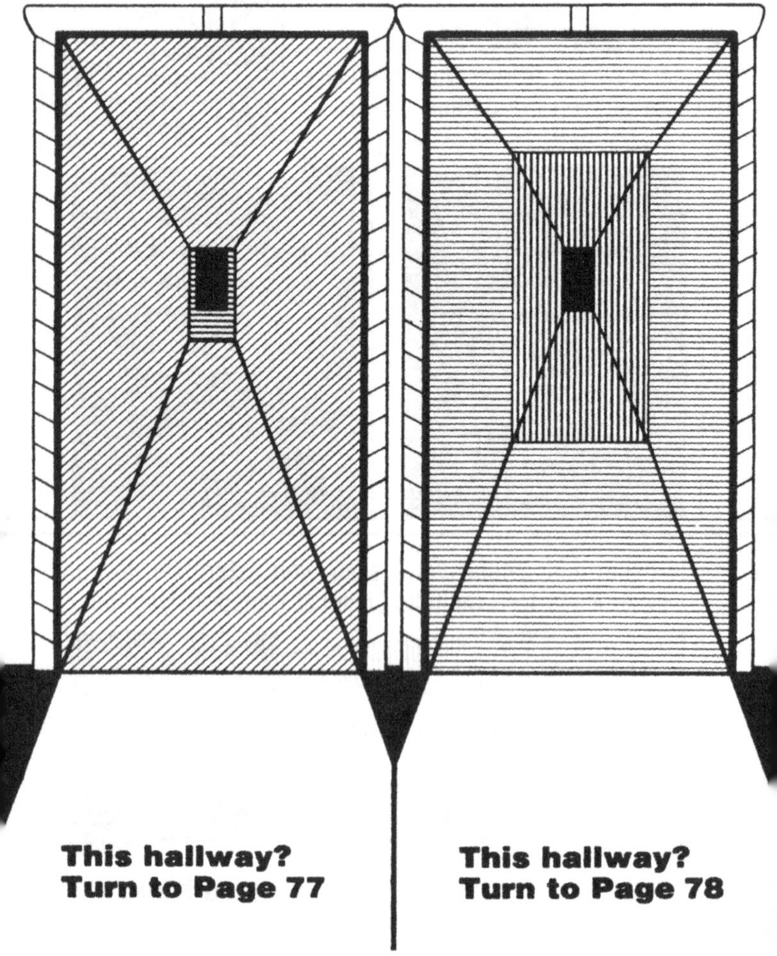

This hallway?
Turn to Page 77

This hallway?
Turn to Page 78

74
Orvat's medallion fits! The statue comes to life!

"Greetings, Starscan!" it says. It is Tavro! He used his mutant powers to "freeze" his body to escape Phatax's robot dogs. They can't track his movements if he is standing still.

= Tavro

Tavro tells you that Prince Quizon is a prisoner in the Royal Palace, and gives you information that will help you find the palace. Suddenly, you hear a strange harsh sound. "Hide," shouts Tavro. Then he freezes again.

You see one of Phatax's robot dogs! You must get back to your ship!

Turn to Page 52

You land safely! But how can you fight a giant that size?

Wait! You remember the snare ring and the stun-gas belt.

Did you bring either with you? Check Page 31.

If you have the snare ring and decide to use it, turn to Page 64

If you have the stun-gas belt, turn to Page 67

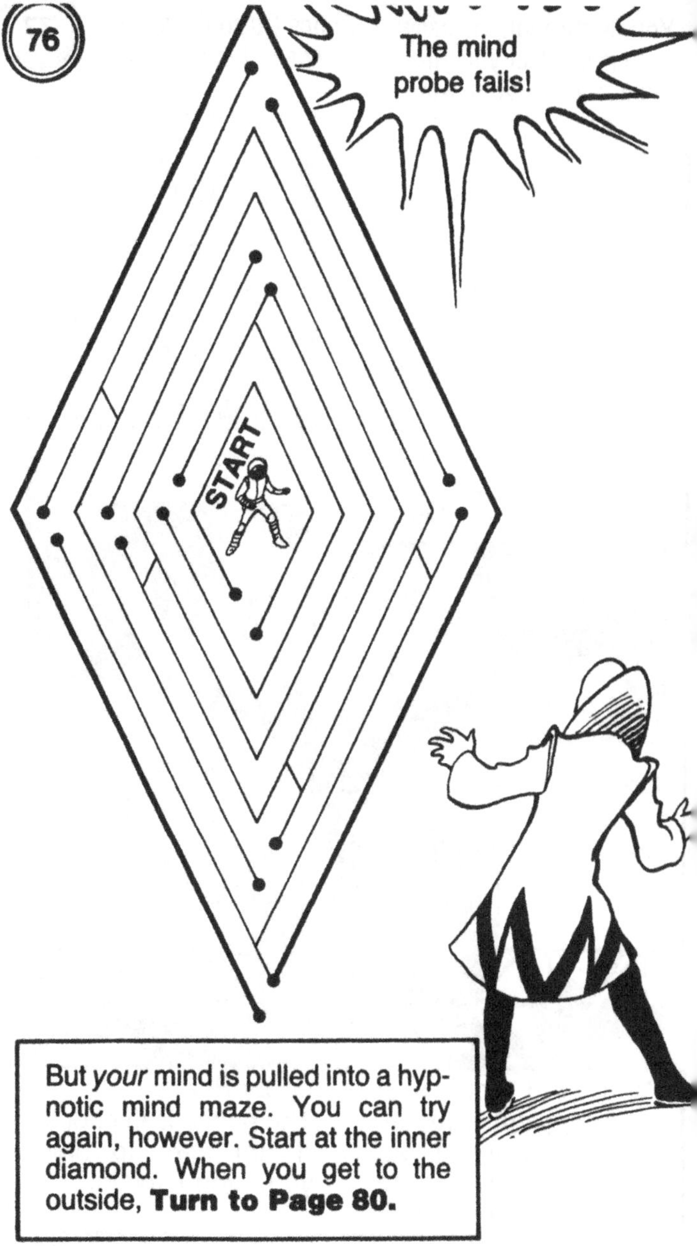
The mind
probe fails!
START

But *your* mind is pulled into a hypnotic mind maze. You can try again, however. Start at the inner diamond. When you get to the outside, **Turn to Page 80.**

You fly through the hallway. Prince Quizon's voice-print is so clear you must be very near, but there is a huge door in your way!

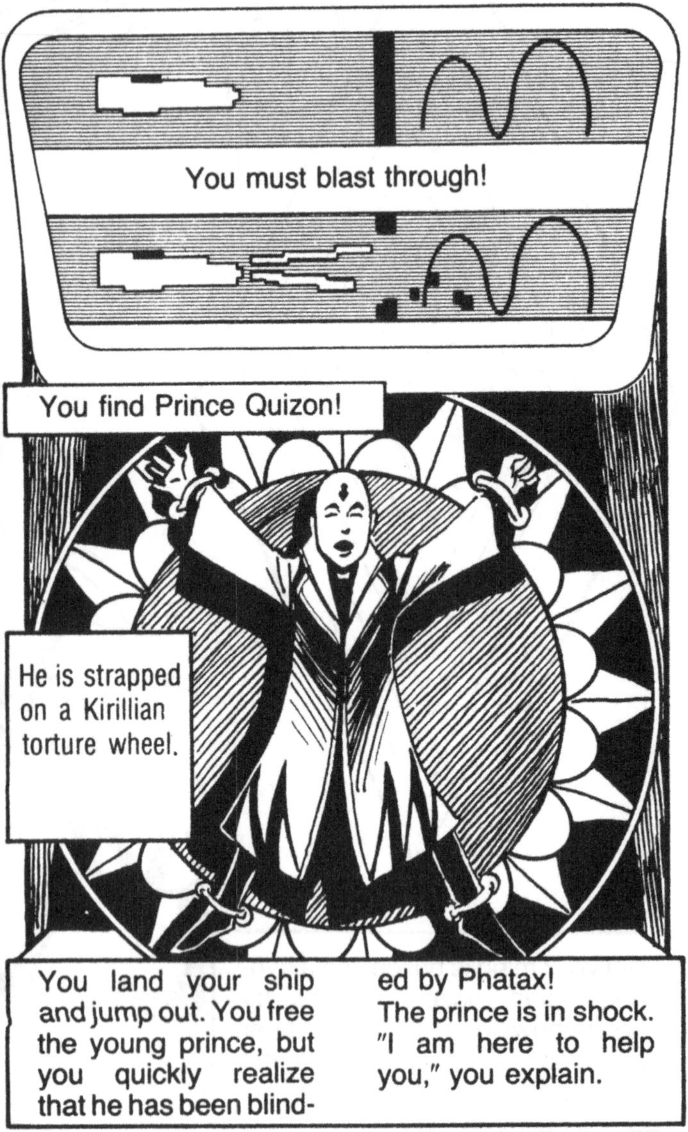
You must blast through!
You find Prince Quizon!
He is strapped on a Kirillian torture wheel.
You land your ship and jump out. You free the young prince, but you quickly realize that he has been blinded by Phatax!
The prince is in shock. "I am here to help you," you explain.

Turn to Page 62

78
You made the wrong choice. Prince Quizon is not here. This is the multidimensional chamber, used to transport people to other planets. Before you can fly out again, your ship accidently triggers the transport device. The transporter beam hits you. You could be transported anywhere!
You are transported to an unknown planet. Unfortunately, the planet you are transported to is about to fall into its sun!
The End

You hurry back to your ship with the jewel Prince Quizon gave you.

IRIDIN

BARENGA

Jungle of Pasquam

Mountains of Krlax

Gelba Plateau

Threefax (Sunward)

MAVORIS

Harquaar

Desert of Orthax

Sampar River

Gaspri Island

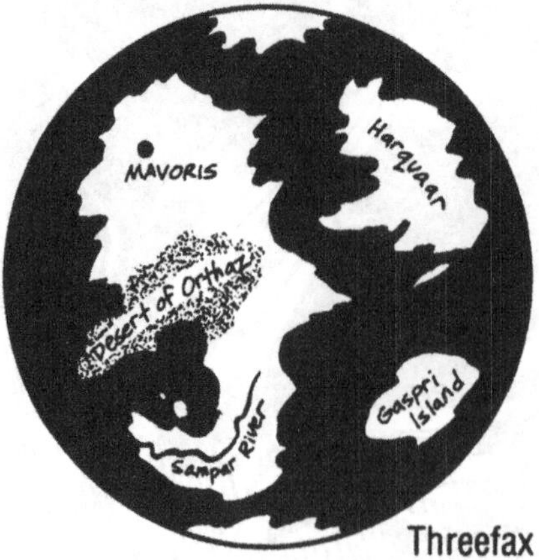

Threefax (Spaceward)

▨ Desert	▨ Mountains
∿ Rivers	■ Oceans	● Cities

Inside the ship, you look at a map of the planet Threefax. Which areas contain sand?

Study the map carefully. Turn to Page 82

Mind Probe
PHATAX ...

BRAGGING ...
THE JEWELS ...
TO UNDERWORLD
DEALERS ... SAND ...
THREEFAX ...
MARKET ...

The mind probe works! You pu
the information together: Pha
tax has taken the jewels to a
sandy region of Threefax, wher
he will sell them to underworl
gem dealers. When you tell thi
to the prince, he nods. He re
members
wha
happened
He reache
into a secre
pocket in his cloa
and pulls out a jewel
"Phatax did not get this one,
he says. "Use it to recover th
other jewels. It is very special
I wish I could see it again!

Turn to Page 8

You must get the blinded prince back to his home planet before taking off after Phatax. Prince Quizon needs rest and proper attention. You quickly take him to the multidimensional chamber of the palace.

Enter the coordinates of Prince Quizon's home planet below. If you don't remember the name of his planet, check Page 3.

Planet Coordinates

Straiten	K5
Kirillia	Z9
Fourton	P2
Zebulax	N3
Alvare	Y1
Metron	W7
Centrax	V7

You activate the chamber and leave Prince Quizon inside. Seconds later, he is on his way home!

Turn to Page 79

The Planet Threefax

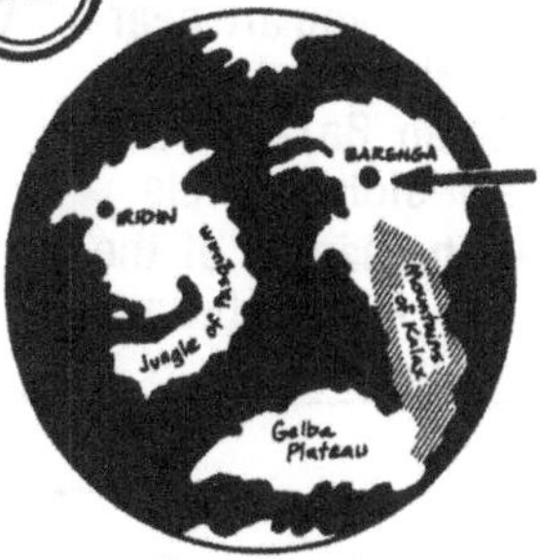

Sunward

Spaceward

The Desert of Orthaz is the best place to look. You must set your ship's course for it. Check the maps above.

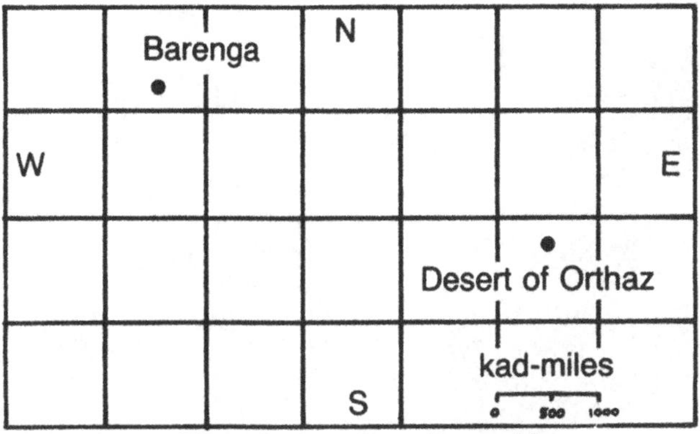

Threefaxian Coordinate Map

Estimate how many kad-miles you will fly:

Now choose your direction.

Northwest?
Turn to Page 84

Southeast?
Turn to Page 86

Your automatic pilot alerts you that you are near the Desert of Orthaz. You put the jewel away. You decide to land at the Zeren Bazaar, the perfect place for Phatax to sell stolen jewels.

You ask your computer for the names of the two biggest jewel merchants in the bazaar.

Now you are ready to land and search for Phatax. Be careful! Trust no one! Phatax may have agents here.

Turn to Page 85

Your ship takes off.
You fly hundreds of kad-miles northwest. You are going in the wrong direction! Suddenly a mountain rises up in front of you. No! It is a living creature! The noise of your ship has woken it up. Before you can get out of its way, the creature blasts you with its icy breath. A cloud of solid ice surrounds your ship. You cannot move! You are frozen!
The End

Your computer tells you that Flodars, a traveling merchant group, are known as the craftiest bargainers in Sector 13. They wear loose-fitting clothing with repeated patterns and vertical lines on them. You decide to pretend you are a merchant from Flodar. You step into your ship's clothworks chamber to get your new clothing.

Select the patterns that will make Flodar-type clothing.

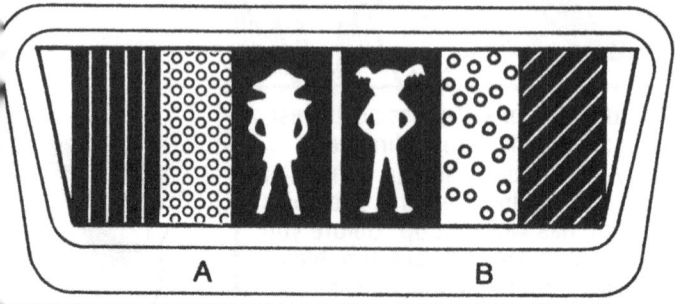

Enter Program A
Turn to Page 87

Enter Program B
Turn to Page 102

Excellent. You set your course southeast for the Desert of Orthaz. Your computer informs you that the distance will be 4,200 kad-miles. You put your ship on automatic pilot.

As you travel, you decide to analyze the jewel that Prince Quizon gave you.

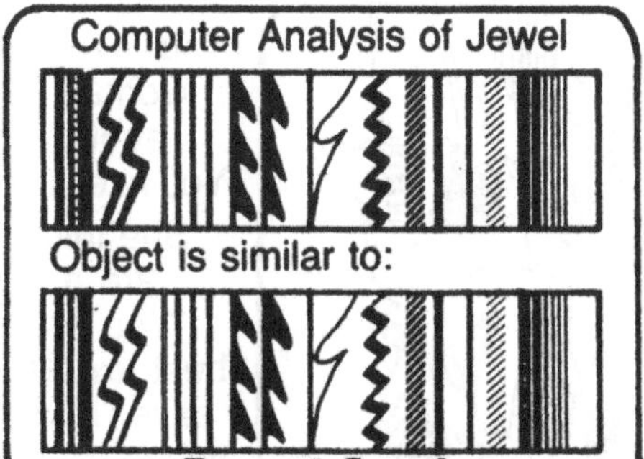

Computer Summary: JEWEL HAS ABILITY TO CONTROL SAND AND CHANGE IT.

Turn to Page 83

You enter the bazaar dressed as a Flodar. Some of the people are giants; some are your size. They respect you. This is a marketplace for people from many worlds, including the underworld!

You overhear a woman talking about jewels. You interrupt her.

She thinks you are a Flodar. "You want the best jewels," she says. "I will take you to Droobil the gem merchant. He has everything!"

Turn to Page 89

88
You fly straight into a cave in-habited by a hungry San-dragon.
The End
Before you can reverse your ship, the Sandragon pounces on you!

You follow the woman through the bazaar. She turns into a dark alleyway and you follow. Suddenly you are blinded by a wall of mirrors! It is a trap!

"I am an agent of Phatax," the woman says. She has a blaster pointed at you. You must protect yourself--but you don't know where to shoot your stun ray.

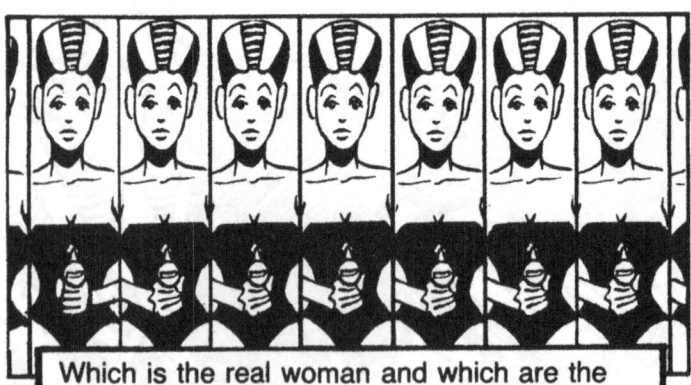

Which is the real woman and which are the mirror images?

Turn to Page 90 when you've figured it out.

90
You fire your stun ray! You know which one she is because she has the gun in her LEFT hand.

The reflected images all have guns in their RIGH hands. Your stun blast knocks her down!

She fires back at you, but her shot goes wild. You freez her with another stun ray. **Turn to Page 9**

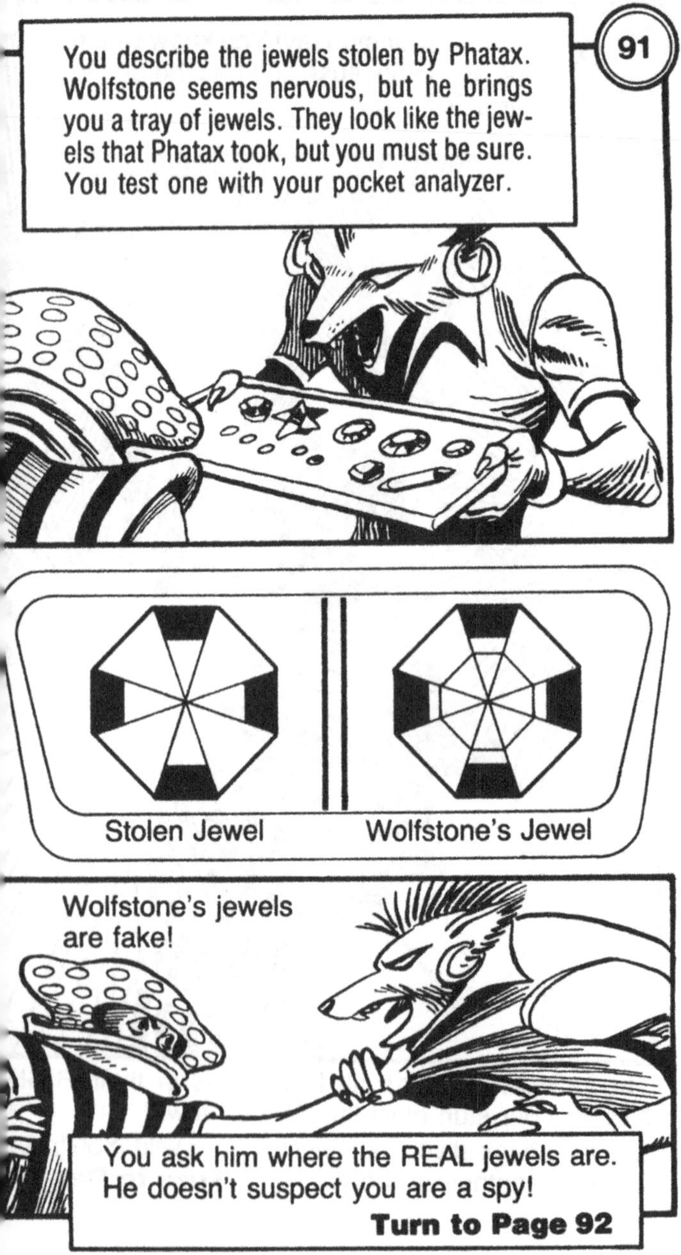
You describe the jewels stolen by Phatax. Wolfstone seems nervous, but he brings you a tray of jewels. They look like the jewels that Phatax took, but you must be sure. You test one with your pocket analyzer.
Stolen Jewel
Wolfstone's Jewel
Wolfstone's jewels are fake!
You ask him where the REAL jewels are. He doesn't suspect you are a spy!
Turn to Page 92

Wolfstone looks around nervously. "You must be Phatax's messenger," he says. "I didn't think he'd send you so fast. Aren't the fakes terrific? You'll be able to sell the Royal Jewels again and again!"
You pretend you are Phatax's messenger. You tell Wolfstone you want to compare the fakes with the originals. Wolfstone brings out the real jewels, and you test them with your analyzer. They *are* real! Suddenly…
A giant foot crashes through the wall!
You dive for a hiding place!
Turn to Page 94

That was a close call! The sleeve of your Flodar costume was singed! You hurry to the first merchant you originally planned to visit—Wolfstone, the famous gem dealer.

You find Wolfstone's shop and enter cautiously. Your Flodar disguise works! Wolfstone welcomes you warmly, and you tell him what kind of jewels you are looking for.

Turn to Page 91

Turn to Page 95

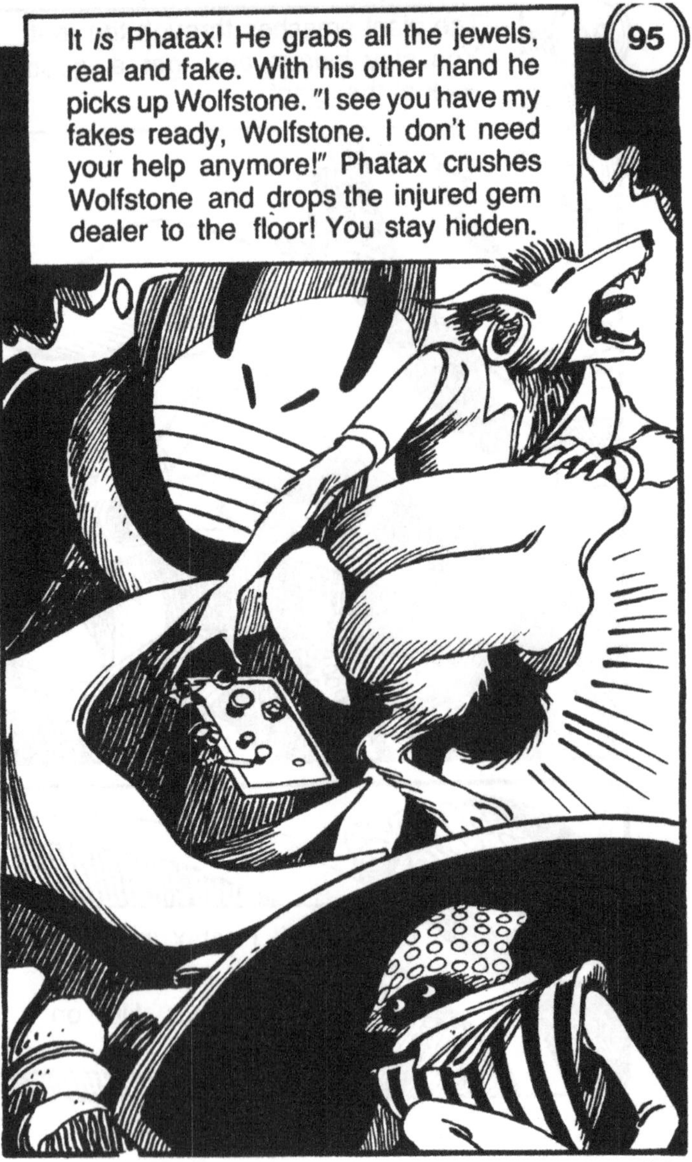
It *is* Phatax! He grabs all the jewels, real and fake. With his other hand he picks up Wolfstone. "I see you have my fakes ready, Wolfstone. I don't need your help anymore!" Phatax crushes Wolfstone and drops the injured gem dealer to the floor! You stay hidden.

Turn to Page 99

You hide outside Phatax's ship. Then you watch Phatax go inside.
The ship takes off.
There is an explosion!
Wait! An escape pod is ejected from the exploding ship.
Phatax!

Your wrist sensor reveals Phatax floating to the ground, safe in his ejection pod. Now you have a better chance of catching him.

Turn to Page 100

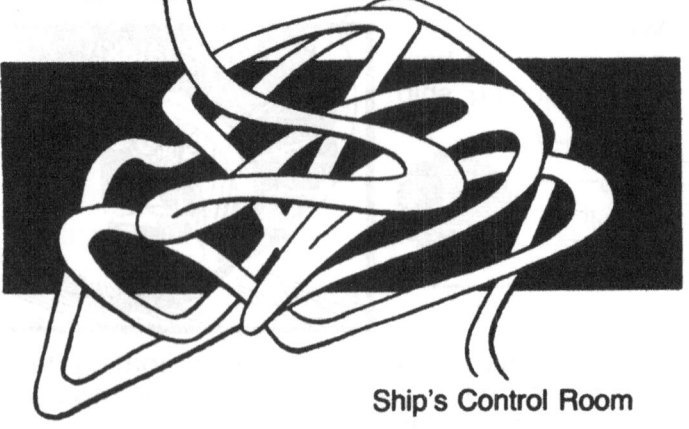

This is Phatax's starcruiser.
The main hatch is locked.
You must crawl in through the air vent.
You must then crawl through the maze of air shafts to get to the control room of Phatax's starcruiser.
Air Vent
Ship's Control Room

Turn to Page 98

You are in the control room of Phatax's starcruiser. You reprogram his ship's computer. If Phatax tries to take off, his ship will be damaged!
Hurry! The scanner shows Phatax returning to his ship. He is not wearing his disguise any longer.
You escape through the ship's air vent. Turn to Page 96

You slip out of Wolfstone's shop. You see Phatax talking to another giant. You must set a trap for Phatax before he can leave the bazaar with the jewels.
You get rid of your awkward Flodar disguise and rush to the bazaar spaceport.

You must find Phatax's ship. But you see two giant Kirillian starcruisers! Which giant ship is Phatax's? Look at your files on Page 7.

Phatax's ship?
Turn to Page 97

Phatax's ship?
Turn to Page 24

100
You rush back to your own ship. You take off and follow the Kirillian!
You fire at his escape pod.
It crashes!
The pod can no longer fly. But it can roll! Phatax rolls away from you at high speed.
Turn to Page 101

Phatax's pod descends into a burrow in the desert. You follow him. The burrow leads to an underground maze of tunnels. These tunnels were made by Sandragons. You must avoid any Sandragons and find Phatax!

Turn to Page 88

Turn to Page 103

102
Your costume
looks ridiculous!

No one would ever believe you are a Flodar. You look more like a Gorond! **Turn back to Page 85 and reprogram the clothworks machine.**

You chase Phatax out of the maze. His giant pod is faster than your ship. But you still can keep him in sight.

You decide to see if you can stop him with your ship's electro-net thrower. You are not sure it will work.

To operate the electro-net, you must connect each A to every other A, connect each B to every other B, and every C to every other C.

        Ⓑ   Ⓒ   Ⓐ

Ⓑ   Ⓑ

Ⓐ   Ⓐ

Ⓒ   Ⓐ

Ⓐ   Ⓑ   Ⓑ

Ⓒ   Ⓒ   Ⓒ

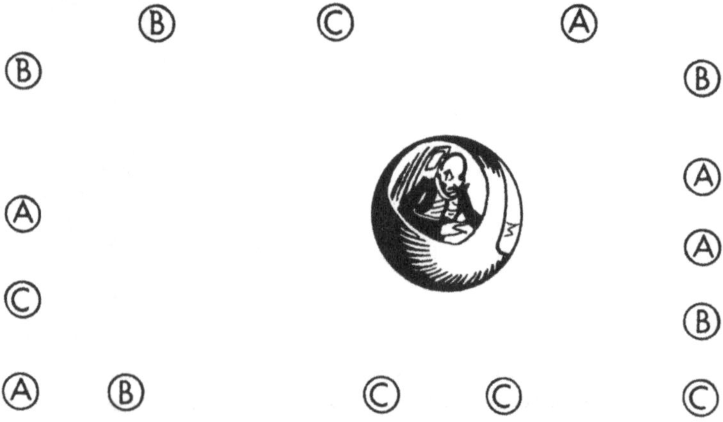

Turn to Page 104

104
The net does not hold the pod. Phatax escapes!

You put on a burst of speed.

You get close enough to fire your ray cannon. You try to blast the pod open!

Turn to Page 106

106
You blast Phatax's escape pod wide open! The Kirillian jumps out of the burning pod with the jewels!
Then, suddenly Phatax disappears! He has turned himself and the jewels invisible!
Turn to Page 109

verything is upside down.

Turn to Page 108

108
Your ship spins out of control.
Safety force field
Ejection pod
You must turn on your ship's safety force field and activate the ejection pod. But you are thrown from the controls!
You must hit the buttons before your ship blows apart!
These buttons?
Turn to Page 111
These buttons?
Turn to Page 56

You fly lower to see if you can see Phatax's footprints.
After you have found them, follow the Kirilian's tracks.
Turn to Page 110

You are able to follow Phatax's footprints. But then you come to a rocky area where the footprints vanish!

You must make Phatax visible by spraying him with positive ions from your ion ray. To make it work, you must match your ship's positive ions to the negative ions in Phatax's invisibile body.

Phatax's negative ions:

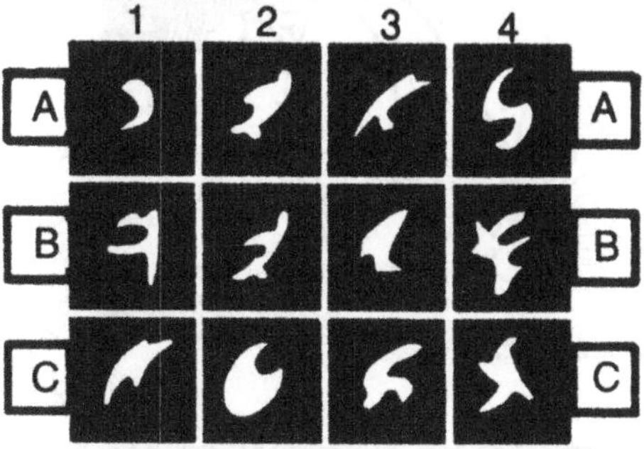

Your ship's positive ion

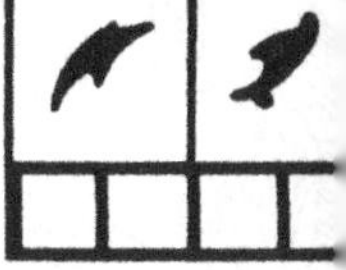

Match positive to negative. Enter your choices. You must match two.

Ion pairs B2 and A3? Turn to Page 14

Ion pairs C1 and A2? Turn to Page 107

You did it! The ejection pod carries you out of your starship safely. You land gently. Your starship lands roughly, but unharmed.
You get out of your pod. You see Phatax climbing onto a strange-looking rock.
Turn to Page 112

The "rock" that Phatax is climbing is actually a huge Sandragon. Its body rises up out of the sand! Phatax gets up on top of the beast and he turns it toward you!

You must find a Sandragon small enough for you to ride.

When you find a Sandragon, turn to Page 115

Your computer told you that the jewel can change the structure of sand. You are surrounded by a desert. You have a plan.

To stop Phatax, you must use the jewel's power over sand. The sun will provide the energy! To best use the sun's energy, you must hold the jewel so that the *least* number of its sides are aimed at the sun.

This way?

Turn to Page 116

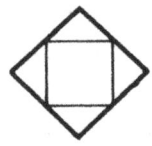

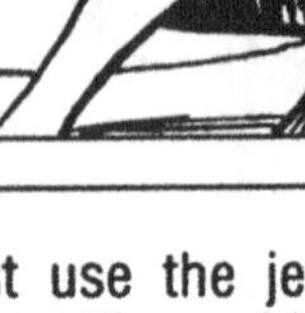

This way?

Turn to Page 14

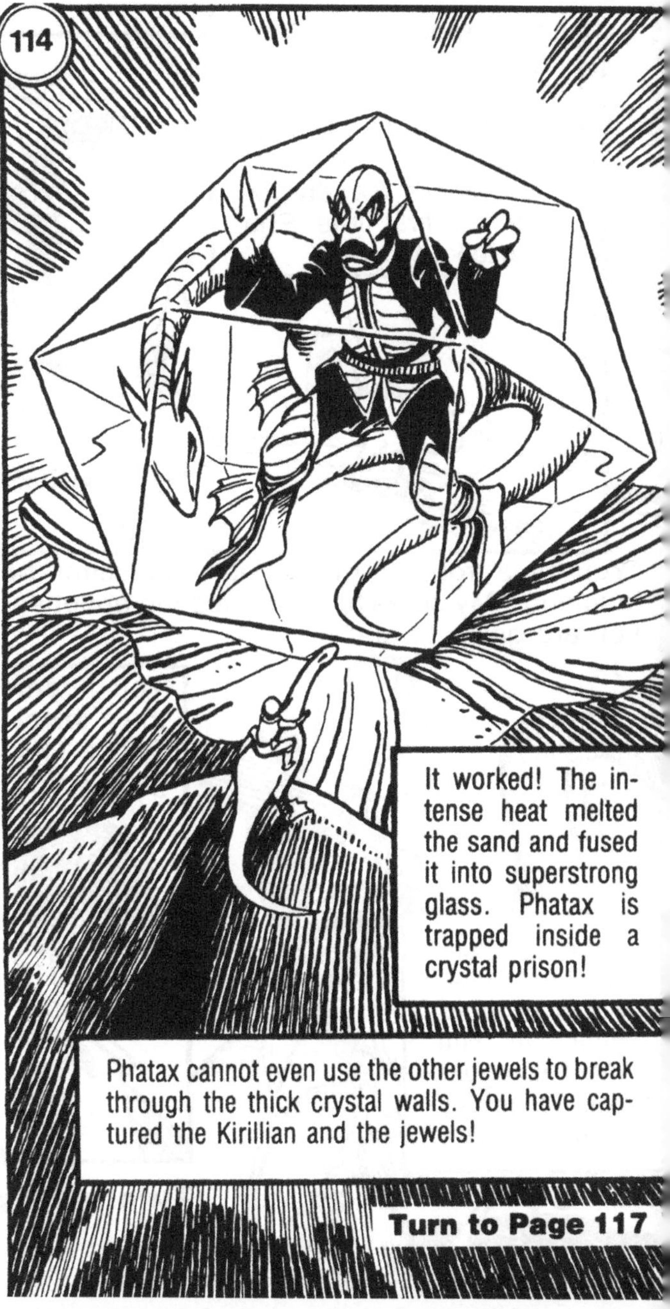
It worked! The intense heat melted the sand and fused it into superstrong glass. Phatax is trapped inside a crystal prison!
Phatax cannot even use the other jewels to break through the thick crystal walls. You have captured the Kirillian and the jewels!

Turn to Page 117

You mount the Sandragon. It bursts out of the sand! You must move quickly. Phatax is charging you on his Sandragon. For the first time, Phatax talks to you.

"You have troubled me enough, Starscan!" he says, laughing. "My spies have warned me about you. Now you are going to die!"

Time is running out. Phatax is 15 times your size. You must use your wits to quickly overcome him!

You remember the jewel that Prince Quizon gave you!

Turn to Page 113

You did it!
The power of the sun blasts through the jewel. It hits the sand around Phatax's feet. The sand changes. It fuses and melts, and then reforms into a hollow crystal that surrounds Phatax.

Turn to Page 114

You can see Phatax screaming at you through the crystal walls, but you cannot hear him! You return quickly to your ship. You send the good news to Prince Quizon's home planet, Alvare. Now you must take Phatax to Alvare and return the jewels to Prince Quizon. The Kirillian will be put on trial for his many crimes.

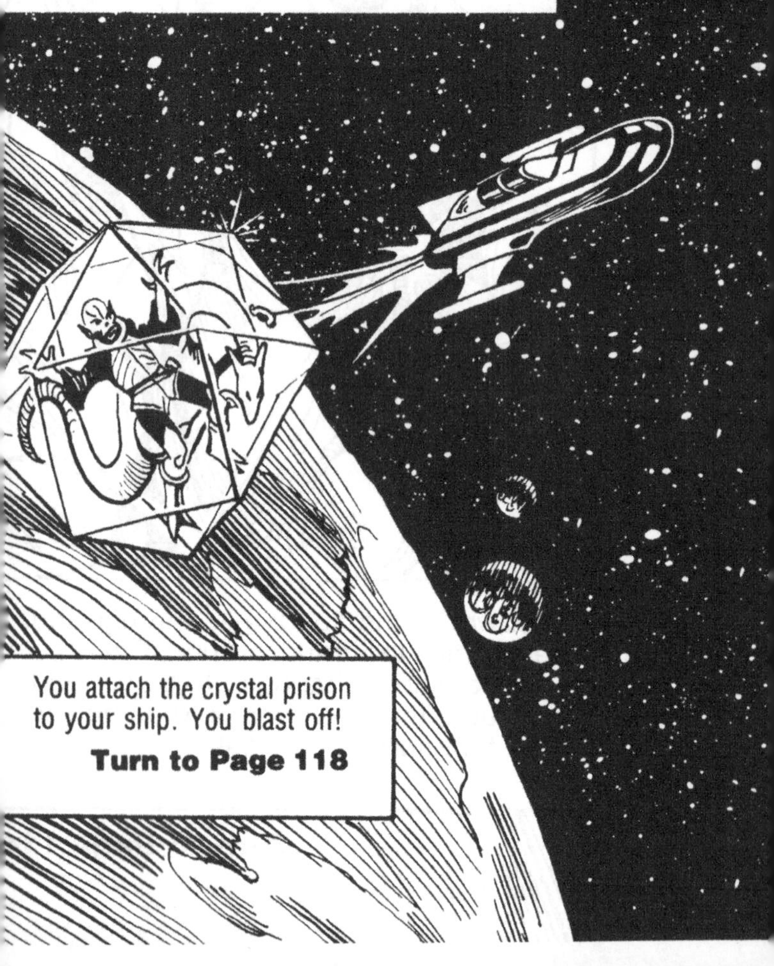

You attach the crystal prison to your ship. You blast off!

Turn to Page 118

You land on Alvare! You turn Phatax over to the police. The Sandragon, which was trapped in the crystal prison with Phatax, is sent to the Interplanetary Zoo.
Prince Quizon's father greets you: "Starscan, you may have any reward you wish for saving my son. What would you like?"
You ask only to see Prince Quizon.

Turn to Page 119

The prince is escorted toward you. He asks if you recovered all of the jewels.

You smile and give the Royal Jewels to Quizon.
Prince Quizon takes two of the jewels out of the bag and raises them to his face.

Turn to Page 120

Prince Quizon lowers his hands. He can see again! He has used the special powers of the jewels to restore his vision.

Your mission is complete. You have proven yourself a first-rate Interplanetary Spy!

Turn to Page 121

Suddenly you hear a loud beeping from your wrist scanner!

You see the face of your commanding officer! She tells you that you must return to base immediately. Another dangerous mission awaits you.

If you enjoyed this book, you can look forward to these other **Be An Interplanetary Spy** books:

#1 FIND THE KIRILLIAN! by McEvoy, Hempel and Wheatley

The ruthless interplanetary criminal Phatax has kidnapped Prince Quizon of Alvare, guardian of the Royal Jewels. You must journey to the planet Threefax, find the Prince and capture Phatax!

#2 THE GALACTIC PIRATE by McEvoy, Hempel and Wheatley

Marko Khen, the Galactic Pirate, has been using his band of criminals to kidnap rare animals from the Interplanetary Zoo. You must find Marko Khen and prevent him from changing the animals into monsters!

#3 ROBOT WORLD by McEvoy, Hempel and Wheatley

Dr. Cyberg, the computer genius, has designed a planet of robots to help humanity. But the robots rebel and Dr. Cyberg disappears! You must track down Dr. Cyberg and face one of the most incredible starships in the galaxy!

#4 SPACE OLYMPICS by Martinez and Pierard

The insidious Gresh, master spy, has threatened to sabotage the galaxy's most famous sports event. You must protect the star of the planet Nez, the super-athlete Andromeda, as she makes her way through the games of the Space Olympics!